PAPERCUTZ SLICES

PERCY JERKSON

& THE OVOLACTOVEGETARIANS

YOU'LL NEVER DIGEST ME, NEVER! THERE'S A LITTLE McKRONOS IN EVERYONE... FOREVER!
MWHAHAHAHA!
AND SO, AN EXTRA LARGE VALUE THREAT WAS UNLEASHED...

PAPERCUTZ™

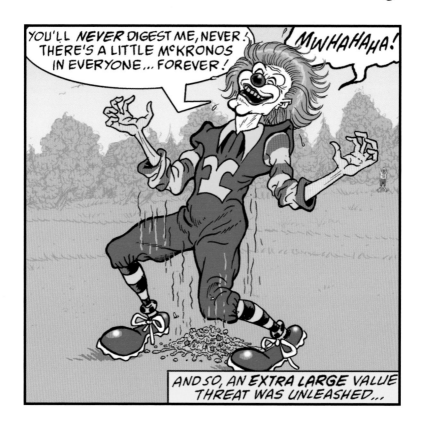

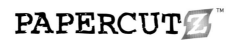

PAPERCUTZ SLICES

Graphic Novels Available from PAPERCUTZ (Who else..?!)

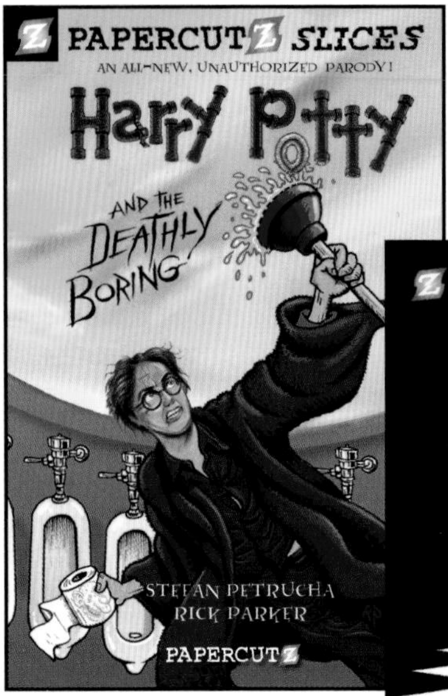
PAPERCUTZ SLICES
AN ALL-NEW, UNAUTHORIZED PARODY!
Harry Potty
AND THE DEATHLY BORING!
STEFAN PETRUCHA
RICK PARKER
PAPERCUTZ

Graphic Novel #1
"Harry Potty and the Deathly Boring"

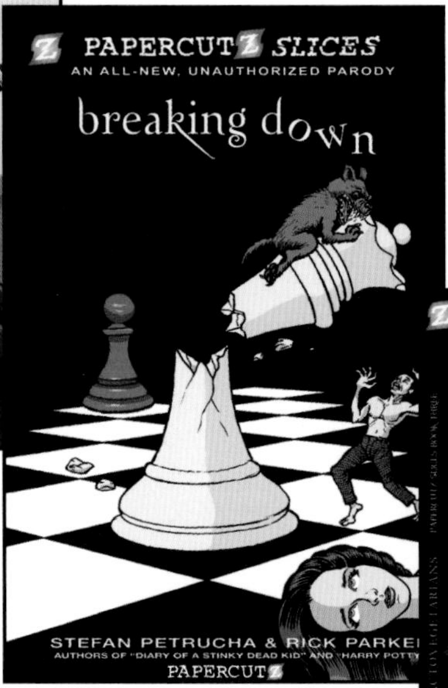
PAPERCUTZ SLICES
AN ALL-NEW, UNAUTHORIZED PARODY
breaking down
STEFAN PETRUCHA &
PAPERCUTZ

Graphic Novel #2
"Breaking Down"

Graphic Novel #3
"Percy Jerkson & The Ovolactovegetarians"

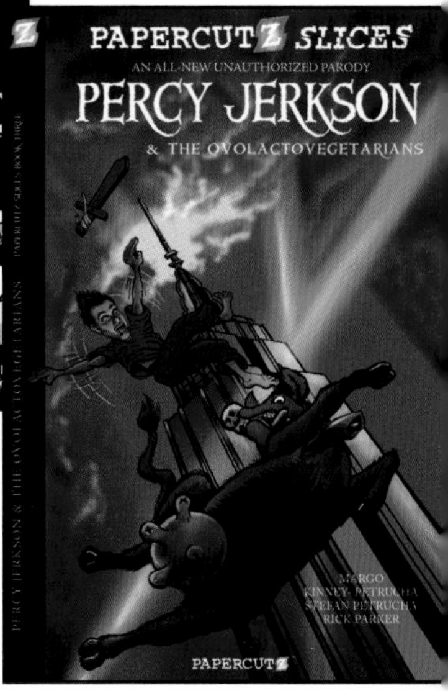
PAPERCUTZ SLICES
AN ALL-NEW UNAUTHORIZED PARODY
PERCY JERKSON
& THE OVOLACTOVEGETARIANS
PAPERCUTZ

PAPERCUTZ SLICES graphic novels are available at booksellers everywhere. At bookstores, comicbook stores, online, out of the trunk in the back of Rick Parker's car, and who knows where else? If you still are unable to find PAPERCUTZ SLICES (probably because it sold out) you can always order directly from Papercutz—but it'll cost you! PAPERCUTZ SLICES is available in paperback for $6.99 each; in hardcover for $10.99 each. But that's not the worst part-- please add $4.00 for postage and handling for the first book, and add $1.00 for each additional book. Going to your favorite bookseller, buying online, or even getting a copy from your local library doesn't seem so bad now, does it? But if you still insist on ordering from Papercutz, and just to make everything just a little bit more complicated, please make your check payable to NBM Publishing. Don't ask why—it's just how it works. Send to: Papercutz, 40 Exchange Place, Ste. 1308, New York, NY 10005 Or call 800 886 1223 (9-6 EST M-F) MC-Visa-Amex accepted

www.papercutz.com

PAPERCUTZ SLICES

#3 PERCY JERKSON

& THE OVOLACTOVEGETARIANS

MARGO KINNEY-PETRUCHA & STEFAN PETRUCHA
Writers
RICK PARKER
Artist

New York

"PERCY JERKSON & THE OVOLACTOVEGETARIANS"

MARGO KINNEY-PETRUCHA & STEFAN PETRUCHA – Writers
RICK PARKER – Artist
RICK PARKER – Colorist
RICK PARKER – Letterer

SHELLY STERNER & CHRIS NELSON
Production

MICHAEL PETRANEK
Associate Editor

JIM SALICRUP
Editor-in-Chief

ISBN: 978-1-59707-264-9 paperback edition
ISBN: 978-1-59707-265-6 hardcover edition

Printed in China
August 2011 by New Era Printing, LTD
Trend Centre, 29-31 Cheung Lee St.
Chaiwan, Hong Kong

First Printing
Distributed by Macmillan

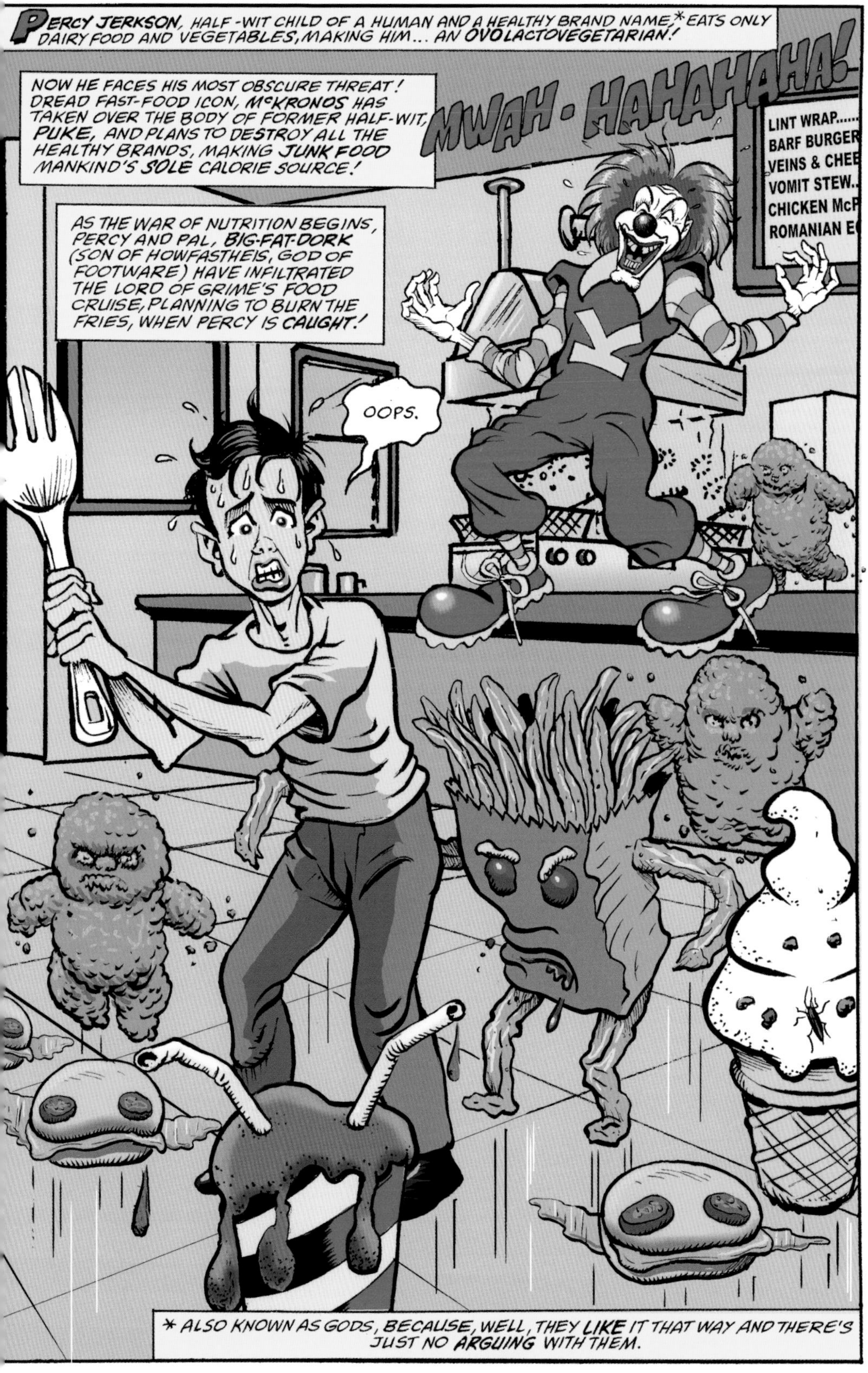
PERCY JERKSON, HALF-WIT CHILD OF A HUMAN AND A HEALTHY BRAND NAME,* EATS ONLY DAIRY FOOD AND VEGETABLES, MAKING HIM... AN OVOLACTOVEGETARIAN!
NOW HE FACES HIS MOST OBSCURE THREAT! DREAD FAST-FOOD ICON, McKRONOS HAS TAKEN OVER THE BODY OF FORMER HALF-WIT, PUKE, AND PLANS TO DESTROY ALL THE HEALTHY BRANDS, MAKING JUNK FOOD MANKIND'S SOLE CALORIE SOURCE!
MWAH-HAHAHAHAHA!
LINT WRAP......
BARF BURGER
VEINS & CHEE
VOMIT STEW..
CHICKEN McP
ROMANIAN E
AS THE WAR OF NUTRITION BEGINS, PERCY AND PAL, BIG-FAT-DORK (SON OF HOWFASTHEIS, GOD OF FOOTWARE) HAVE INFILTRATED THE LORD OF GRIME'S FOOD CRUISE, PLANNING TO BURN THE FRIES, WHEN PERCY IS CAUGHT!
OOPS.
* ALSO KNOWN AS GODS, BECAUSE, WELL, THEY LIKE IT THAT WAY AND THERE'S JUST NO ARGUING WITH THEM.

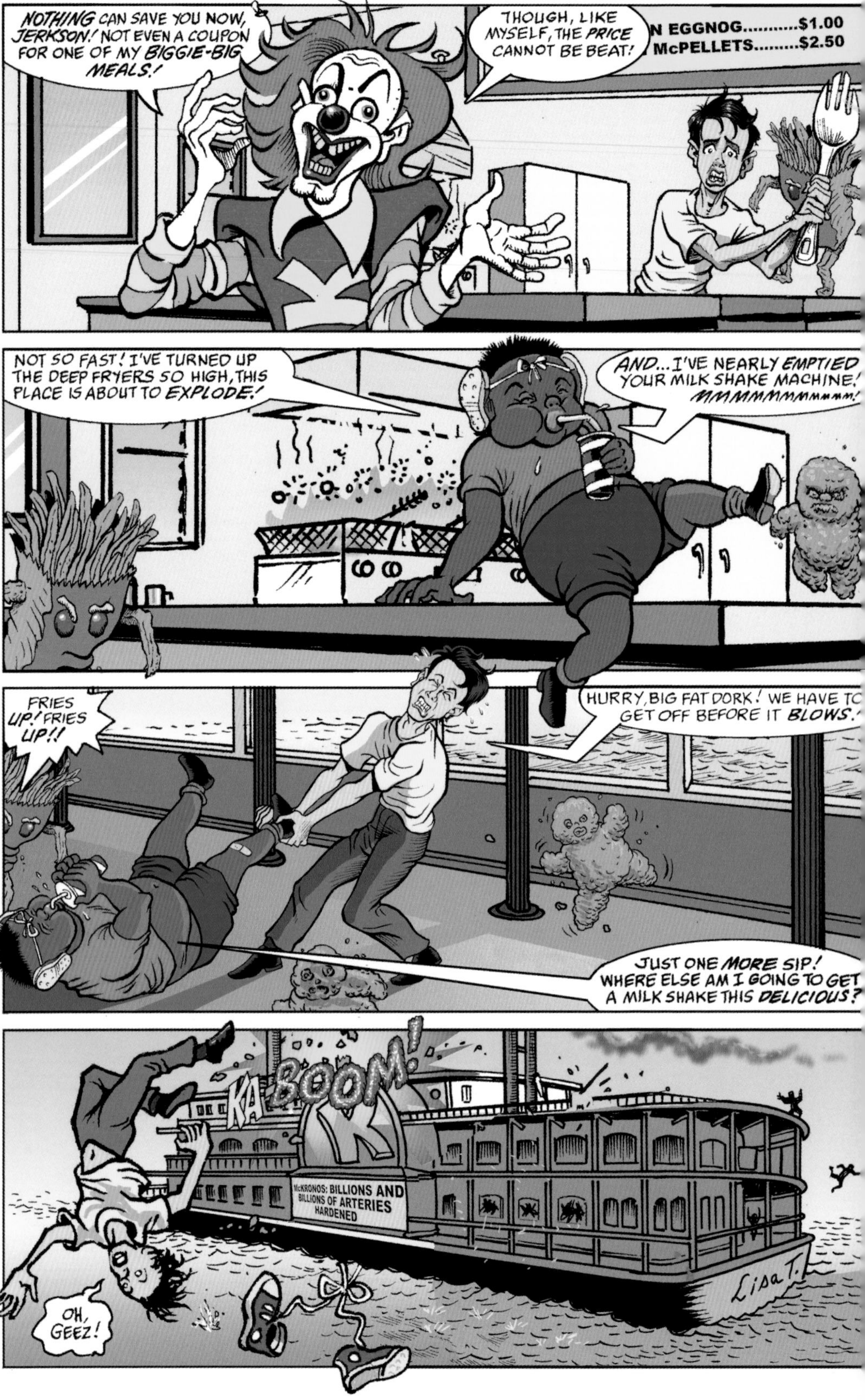
NOTHING CAN SAVE YOU NOW, JERKSON! NOT EVEN A COUPON FOR ONE OF MY BIGGIE-BIG MEALS!
THOUGH, LIKE MYSELF, THE PRICE CANNOT BE BEAT!
N EGGNOG..........$1.00
McPELLETS.........$2.50
NOT SO FAST! I'VE TURNED UP THE DEEP FRYERS SO HIGH, THIS PLACE IS ABOUT TO EXPLODE!
AND...I'VE NEARLY EMPTIED YOUR MILK SHAKE MACHINE! MMMMMMMmmmm!
FRIES UP! FRIES UP!!
HURRY, BIG FAT DORK! WE HAVE TO GET OFF BEFORE IT BLOWS!
JUST ONE MORE SIP! WHERE ELSE AM I GOING TO GET A MILK SHAKE THIS DELICIOUS?
KA BOOM!
McKRONOS: BILLIONS AND BILLIONS OF ARTERIES HARDENED
OH, GEEZ!
Lisa T.

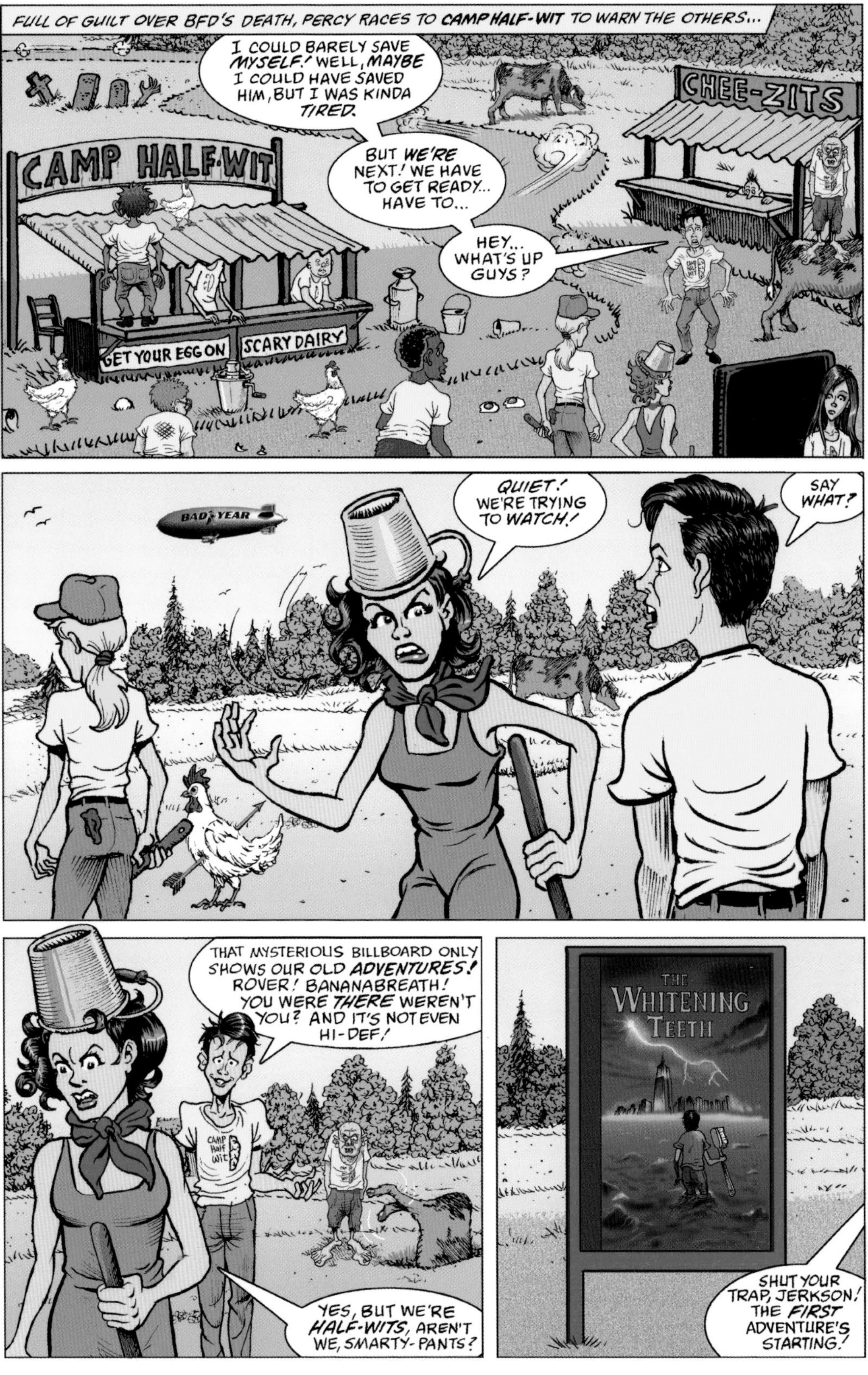
FULL OF GUILT OVER BFD'S DEATH, PERCY RACES TO CAMP HALF-WIT TO WARN THE OTHERS...
I COULD BARELY SAVE MYSELF! WELL, MAYBE I COULD HAVE SAVED HIM, BUT I WAS KINDA TIRED.
BUT WE'RE NEXT! WE HAVE TO GET READY... HAVE TO...
HEY... WHAT'S UP GUYS?
CAMP HALF-WIT
CHEE-ZITS
GET YOUR EGG ON
SCARY DAIRY
BAD YEAR
QUIET! WE'RE TRYING TO WATCH!
SAY WHAT?
THAT MYSTERIOUS BILLBOARD ONLY SHOWS OUR OLD ADVENTURES! ROVER! BANANABREATH! YOU WERE THERE WEREN'T YOU? AND IT'S NOT EVEN HI-DEF!
YES, BUT WE'RE HALF-WITS, AREN'T WE, SMARTY-PANTS?
THE WHITENING TEETH
SHUT YOUR TRAP, JERKSON! THE FIRST ADVENTURE'S STARTING!

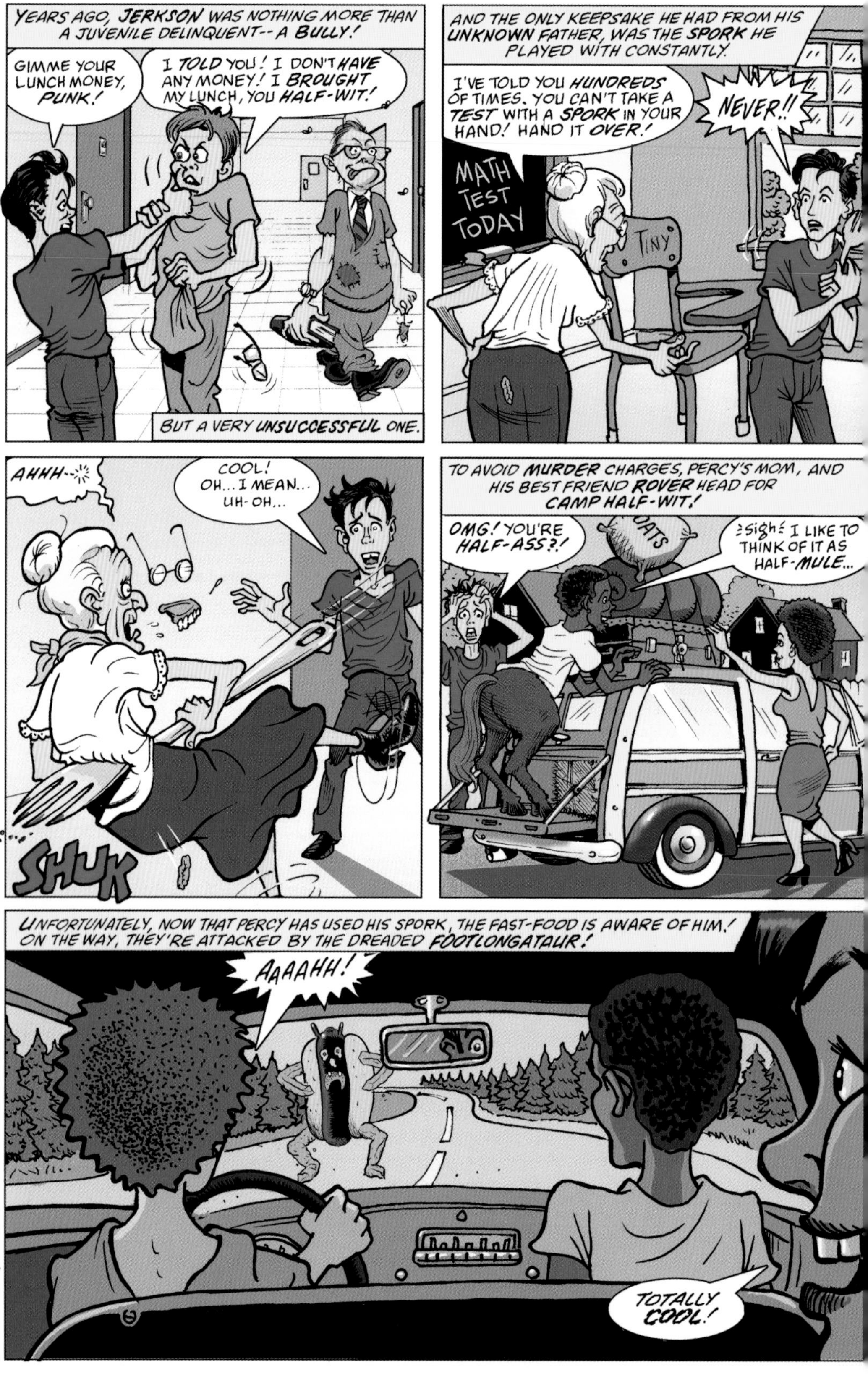
YEARS AGO, JERKSON WAS NOTHING MORE THAN A JUVENILE DELINQUENT--A BULLY!
GIMME YOUR LUNCH MONEY, PUNK!
I TOLD YOU! I DON'T HAVE ANY MONEY! I BROUGHT MY LUNCH, YOU HALF-WIT!
BUT A VERY UNSUCCESSFUL ONE.
AND THE ONLY KEEPSAKE HE HAD FROM HIS UNKNOWN FATHER, WAS THE SPORK HE PLAYED WITH CONSTANTLY.
I'VE TOLD YOU HUNDREDS OF TIMES. YOU CAN'T TAKE A TEST WITH A SPORK IN YOUR HAND! HAND IT OVER!
NEVER!!
MATH TEST TODAY
TINY
AHHH--
COOL! OH... I MEAN... UH-OH...
SHUK
TO AVOID MURDER CHARGES, PERCY'S MOM, AND HIS BEST FRIEND ROVER HEAD FOR CAMP HALF-WIT!
OMG! YOU'RE HALF-ASS?!
OATS
sigh I LIKE TO THINK OF IT AS HALF-MULE...
UNFORTUNATELY, NOW THAT PERCY HAS USED HIS SPORK, THE FAST-FOOD IS AWARE OF HIM! ON THE WAY, THEY'RE ATTACKED BY THE DREADED FOOTLONGATAUR!
AAAAHH!
TOTALLY COOL!

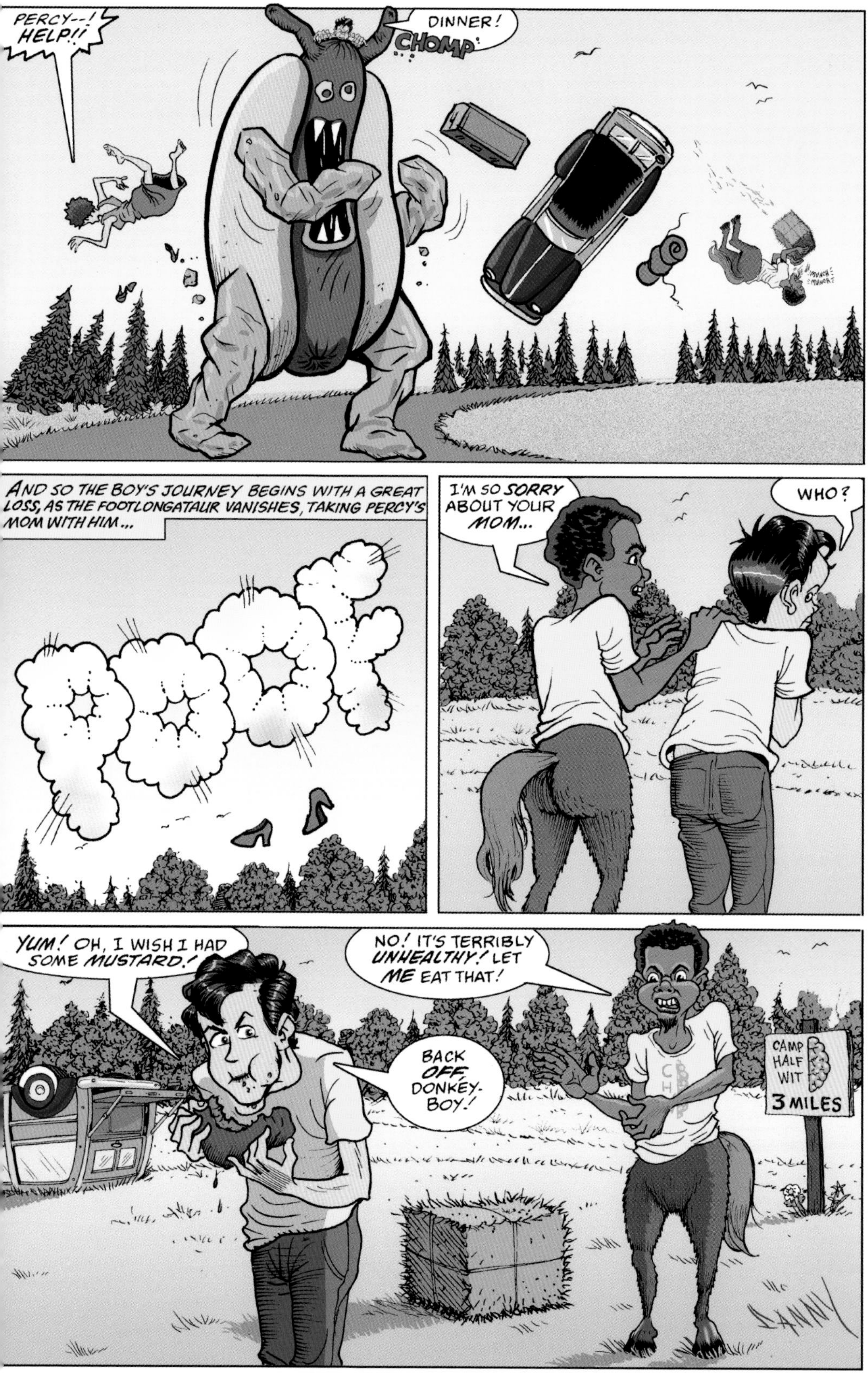
PERCY--! HELP!!
DINNER!
CHOMP
MUNCH
MUNCH
AND SO THE BOY'S JOURNEY BEGINS WITH A GREAT LOSS, AS THE FOOTLONGATAUR VANISHES, TAKING PERCY'S MOM WITH HIM...
POOF
I'M SO SORRY ABOUT YOUR MOM...
WHO?
YUM! OH, I WISH I HAD SOME MUSTARD!
NO! IT'S TERRIBLY UNHEALTHY! LET ME EAT THAT!
BACK OFF, DONKEY-BOY!
CAMP HALF WIT
3 MILES
DANNY

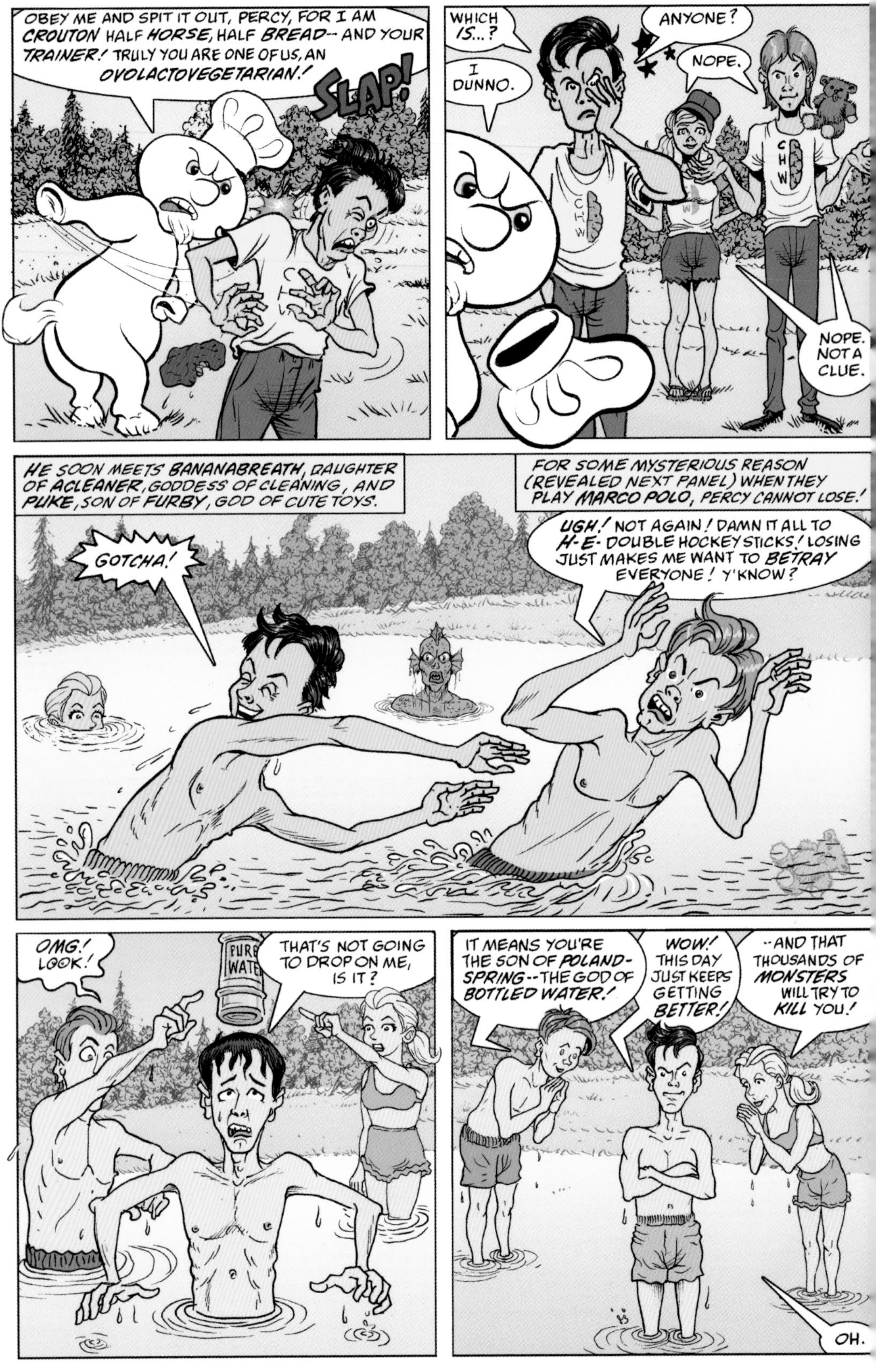
OBEY ME AND SPIT IT OUT, PERCY, FOR I AM CROUTON HALF HORSE, HALF BREAD-- AND YOUR TRAINER! TRULY YOU ARE ONE OF US, AN OVOLACTOVEGETARIAN!
SLAP!
WHICH IS...?
I DUNNO.
ANYONE?
NOPE.
NOPE. NOT A CLUE.
HE SOON MEETS BANANABREATH, DAUGHTER OF ACLEANER, GODDESS OF CLEANING, AND PUKE, SON OF FURBY, GOD OF CUTE TOYS.
FOR SOME MYSTERIOUS REASON (REVEALED NEXT PANEL) WHEN THEY PLAY MARCO POLO, PERCY CANNOT LOSE!
GOTCHA!
UGH! NOT AGAIN! DAMN IT ALL TO H-E- DOUBLE HOCKEY STICKS! LOSING JUST MAKES ME WANT TO BETRAY EVERYONE! Y'KNOW?
OMG! LOOK!
PURE WATER
THAT'S NOT GOING TO DROP ON ME, IS IT?
IT MEANS YOU'RE THE SON OF POLAND-SPRING--THE GOD OF BOTTLED WATER!
WOW! THIS DAY JUST KEEPS GETTING BETTER!
--AND THAT THOUSANDS OF MONSTERS WILL TRY TO KILL YOU!
OH.

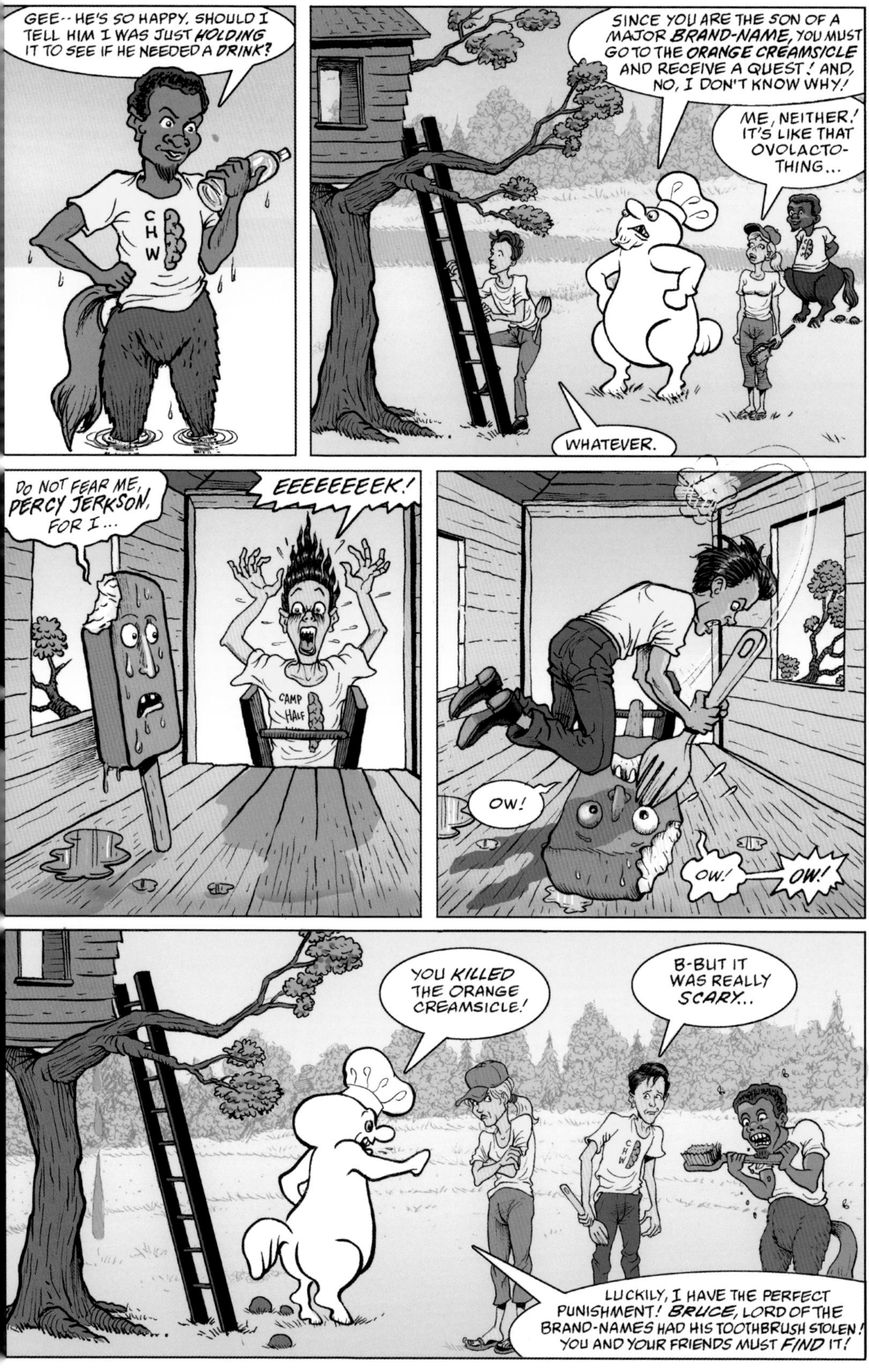
GEE-- HE'S SO HAPPY. SHOULD I TELL HIM I WAS JUST *HOLDING* IT TO SEE IF HE NEEDED A *DRINK*?
SINCE YOU ARE THE SON OF A MAJOR *BRAND-NAME*, YOU MUST GO TO THE *ORANGE CREAMSICLE* AND RECEIVE A QUEST! AND, NO, I DON'T KNOW WHY!
ME, NEITHER! IT'S LIKE THAT OVOLACTO-THING...
WHATEVER.
DO NOT FEAR ME, *PERCY JERKSON*, FOR I...
EEEEEEEEK!
CAMP HALF
OW!
OW!
OW!
YOU *KILLED* THE ORANGE CREAMSICLE!
B-BUT IT WAS REALLY *SCARY*...
LUCKILY, I HAVE THE PERFECT PUNISHMENT! *BRUCE*, LORD OF THE BRAND-NAMES HAD HIS TOOTHBRUSH STOLEN! YOU AND YOUR FRIENDS MUST *FIND* IT!

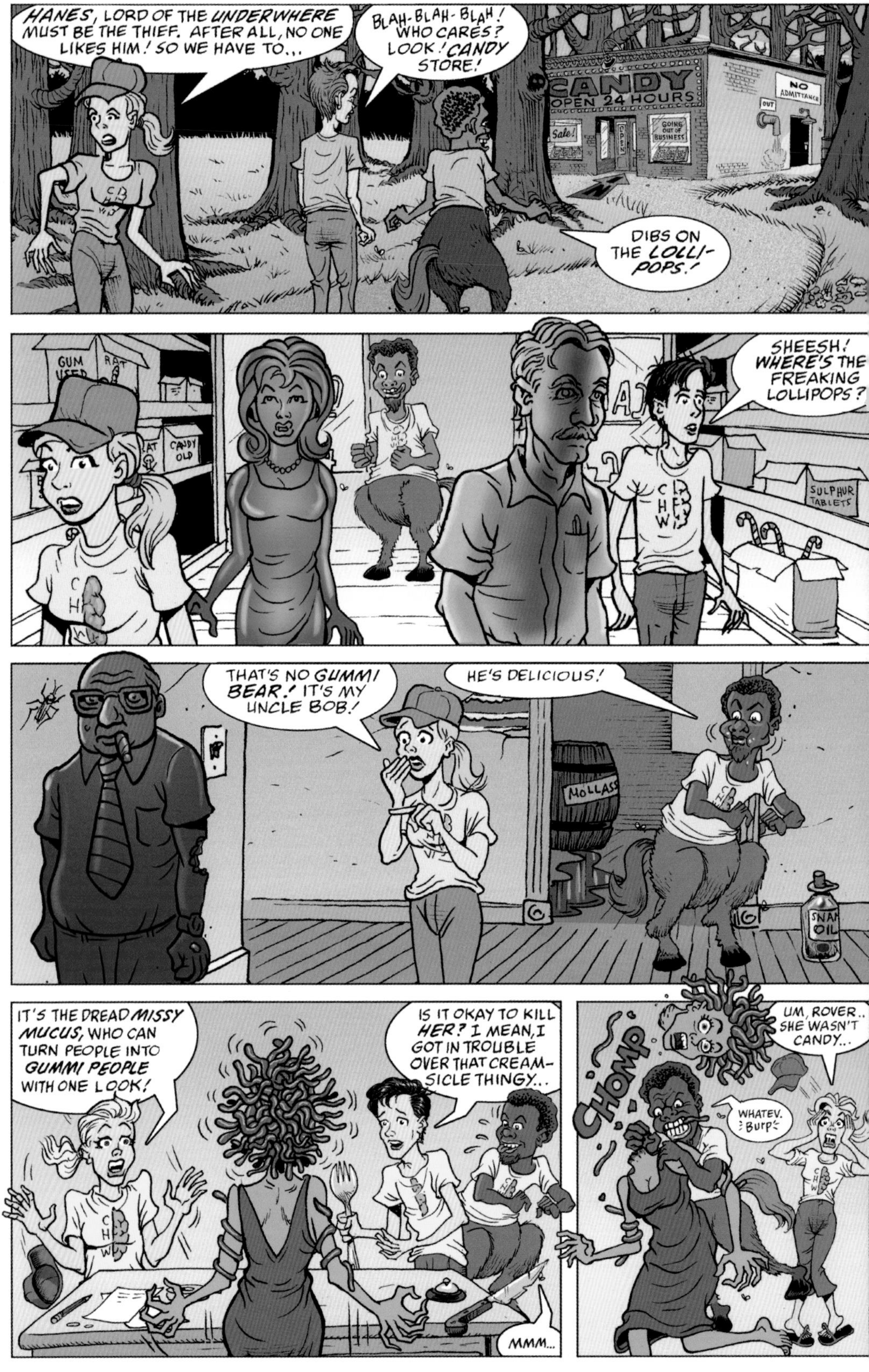
HANES, LORD OF THE UNDERWHERE MUST BE THE THIEF. AFTER ALL, NO ONE LIKES HIM! SO WE HAVE TO...
BLAH-BLAH-BLAH! WHO CARES? LOOK! CANDY STORE!
CANDY
OPEN 24 HOURS
NO ADMITTANCE
OUT
Sale!
OPEN
GOING OUT OF BUSINESS
DIBS ON THE LOLLI-POPS!
SHEESH! WHERE'S THE FREAKING LOLLIPOPS?
GUM USED
CANDY OLD
SULPHUR TABLETS
THAT'S NO GUMMI BEAR! IT'S MY UNCLE BOB!
HE'S DELICIOUS!
MOLLASS
IT'S THE DREAD MISSY MUCUS, WHO CAN TURN PEOPLE INTO GUMMI PEOPLE WITH ONE LOOK!
IS IT OKAY TO KILL HER? I MEAN, I GOT IN TROUBLE OVER THAT CREAM-SICLE THING...
MMM...
CHOMP
UM, ROVER.. SHE WASN'T CANDY...
WHATEV. Burp

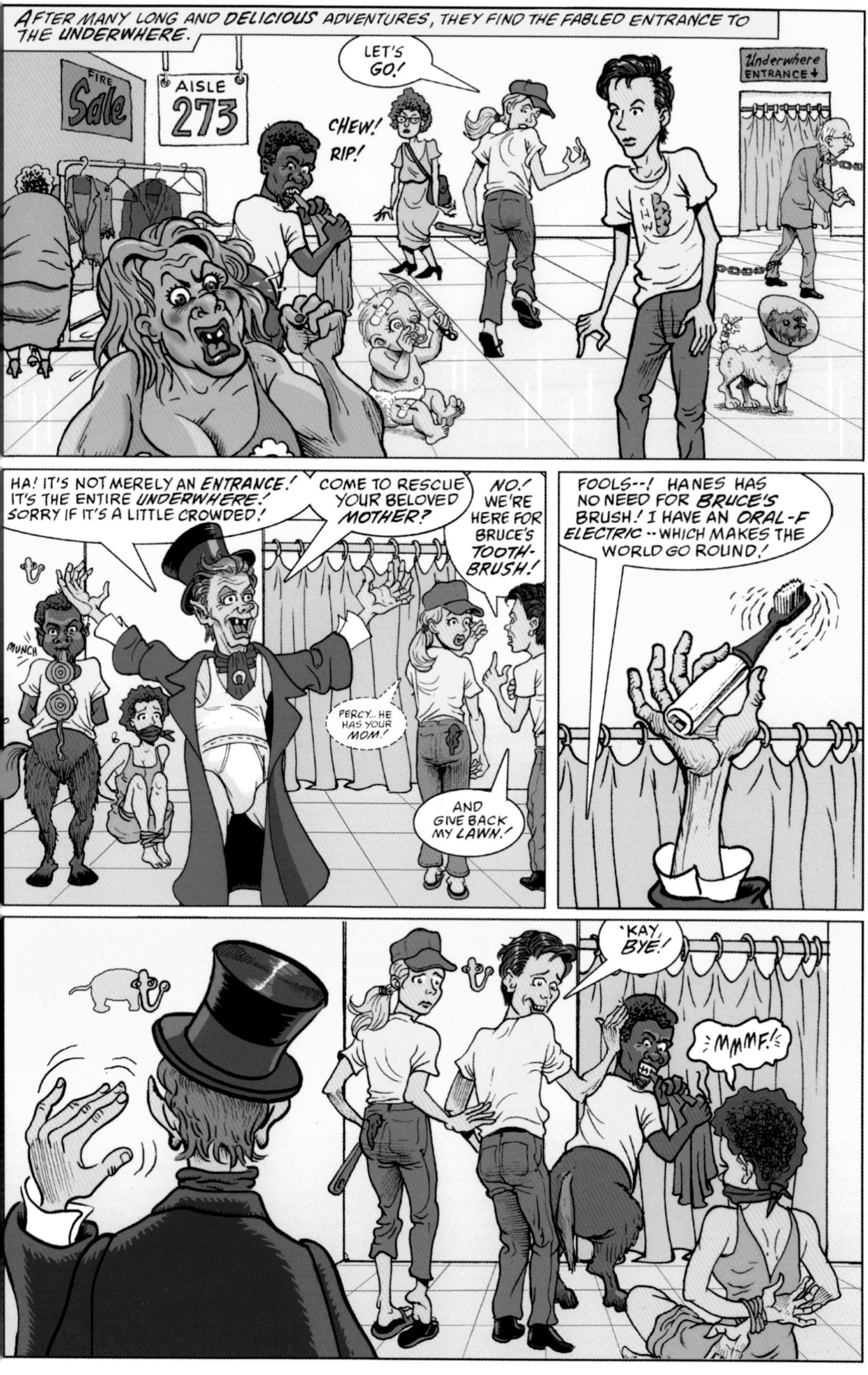
AFTER MANY LONG AND DELICIOUS ADVENTURES, THEY FIND THE FABLED ENTRANCE TO THE UNDERWHERE.
FIRE Sale
AISLE 273
LET'S GO!
CHEW! RIP!
Underwhere ENTRANCE
CHW
HA! IT'S NOT MERELY AN ENTRANCE! IT'S THE ENTIRE UNDERWHERE! SORRY IF IT'S A LITTLE CROWDED!
COME TO RESCUE YOUR BELOVED MOTHER?
NO! WE'RE HERE FOR BRUCE'S TOOTH-BRUSH!
MUNCH
PERCY.. HE HAS YOUR MOM!
AND GIVE BACK MY LAWN!
FOOLS--! HANES HAS NO NEED FOR BRUCE'S BRUSH! I HAVE AN ORAL-F ELECTRIC -- WHICH MAKES THE WORLD GO ROUND!
'KAY, BYE!
MMMF!

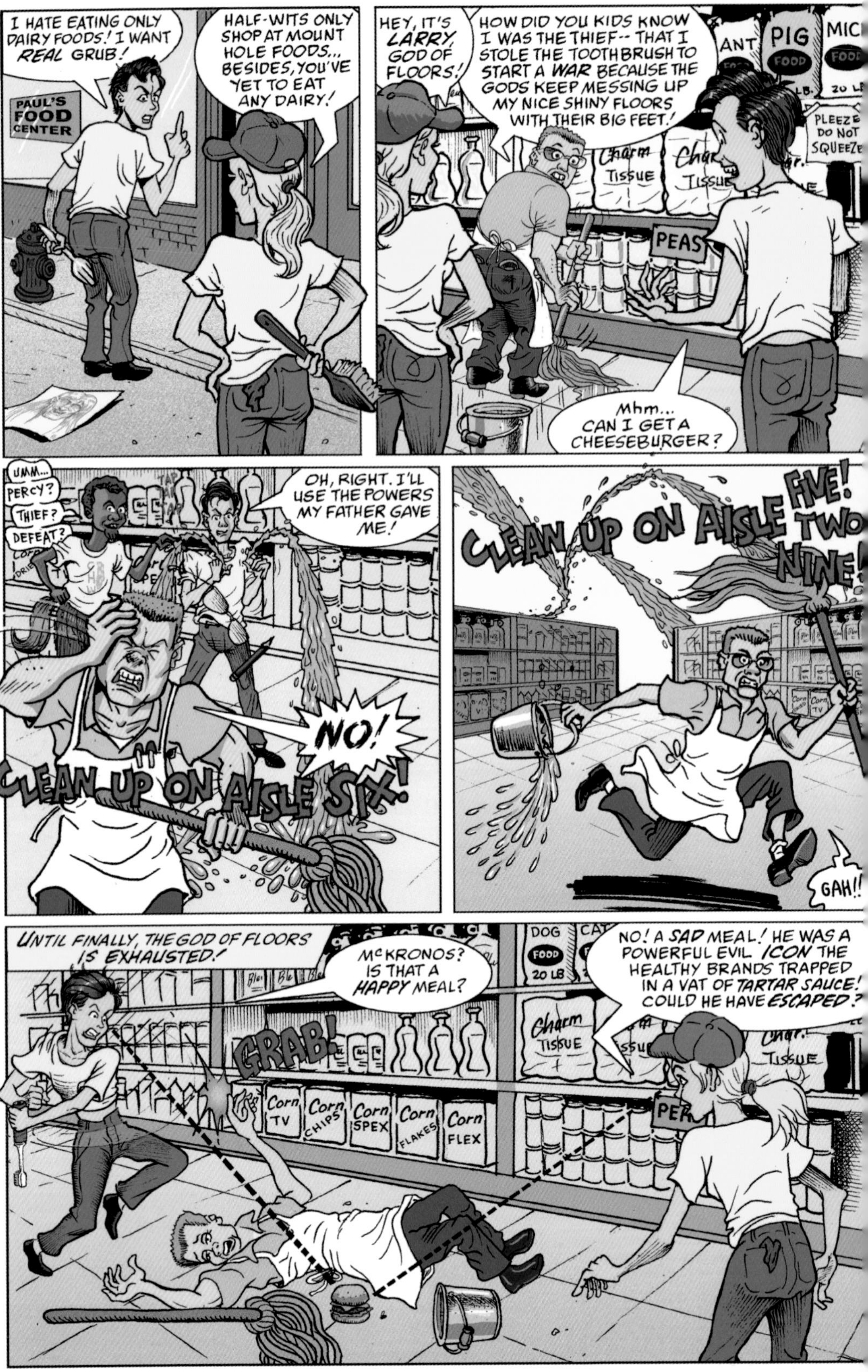
I HATE EATING ONLY DAIRY FOODS! I WANT REAL GRUB!
PAUL'S FOOD CENTER
HALF-WITS ONLY SHOP AT MOUNT HOLE FOODS... BESIDES, YOU'VE YET TO EAT ANY DAIRY!
HEY, IT'S LARRY, GOD OF FLOORS!
HOW DID YOU KIDS KNOW I WAS THE THIEF-- THAT I STOLE THE TOOTHBRUSH TO START A WAR BECAUSE THE GODS KEEP MESSING UP MY NICE SHINY FLOORS WITH THEIR BIG FEET!
PIG FOOD
PLEEZE DO NOT SQUEEZE
Charm TISSUE
PEAS
Mhm... CAN I GET A CHEESEBURGER?
UMM... PERCY? THIEF? DEFEAT?
OH, RIGHT. I'LL USE THE POWERS MY FATHER GAVE ME!
NO!
CLEAN UP ON AISLE SIX!
CLEAN UP ON AISLE FIVE! TWO! NINE!
GAH!!
UNTIL FINALLY, THE GOD OF FLOORS IS EXHAUSTED!
McKRONOS? IS THAT A HAPPY MEAL?
DOG FOOD 20 LB
NO! A SAD MEAL! HE WAS A POWERFUL EVIL ICON THE HEALTHY BRANDS TRAPPED IN A VAT OF TARTAR SAUCE! COULD HE HAVE ESCAPED?
GRAB!
Corn TV
Corn CHIPS
Corn SPEX
Corn FLAKES
Corn FLEX
Charm TISSUE

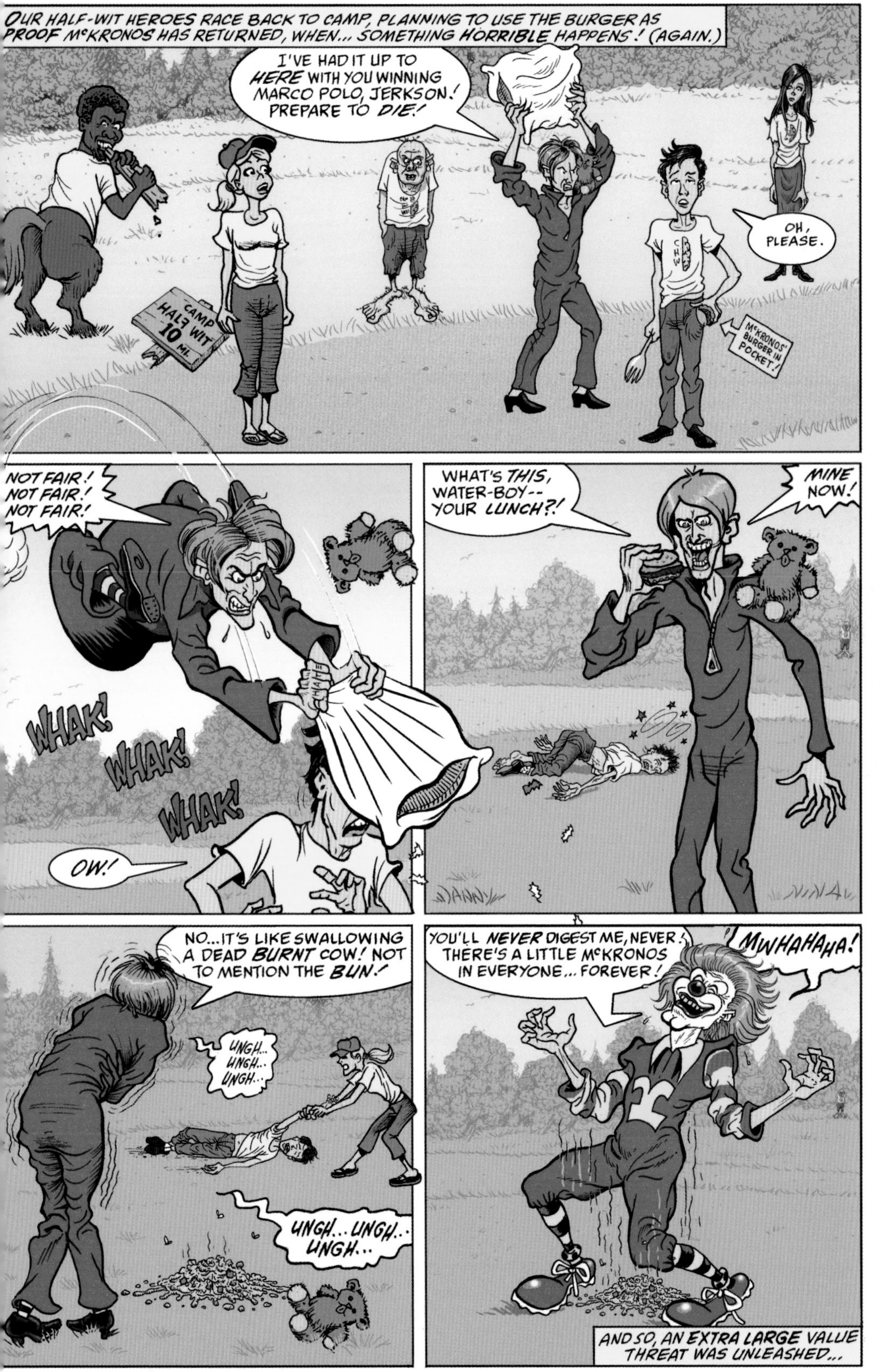
OUR HALF-WIT HEROES RACE BACK TO CAMP, PLANNING TO USE THE BURGER AS PROOF McKRONOS HAS RETURNED, WHEN... SOMETHING HORRIBLE HAPPENS! (AGAIN.)
I'VE HAD IT UP TO HERE WITH YOU WINNING MARCO POLO, JERKSON! PREPARE TO DIE!
OH, PLEASE.
CAMP HALF WIT 10 MI.
McKRONOS' BURGER IN POCKET!
NOT FAIR! NOT FAIR! NOT FAIR!
WHAK! WHAK! WHAK!
OW!
WHAT'S THIS, WATER-BOY-- YOUR LUNCH?!
MINE NOW!
NO... IT'S LIKE SWALLOWING A DEAD BURNT COW! NOT TO MENTION THE BUN!
UNGH... UNGH... UNGH...
UNGH... UNGH... UNGH...
YOU'LL NEVER DIGEST ME, NEVER! THERE'S A LITTLE McKRONOS IN EVERYONE... FOREVER!
MWHAHAHAHA!
AND SO, AN EXTRA LARGE VALUE THREAT WAS UNLEASHED...

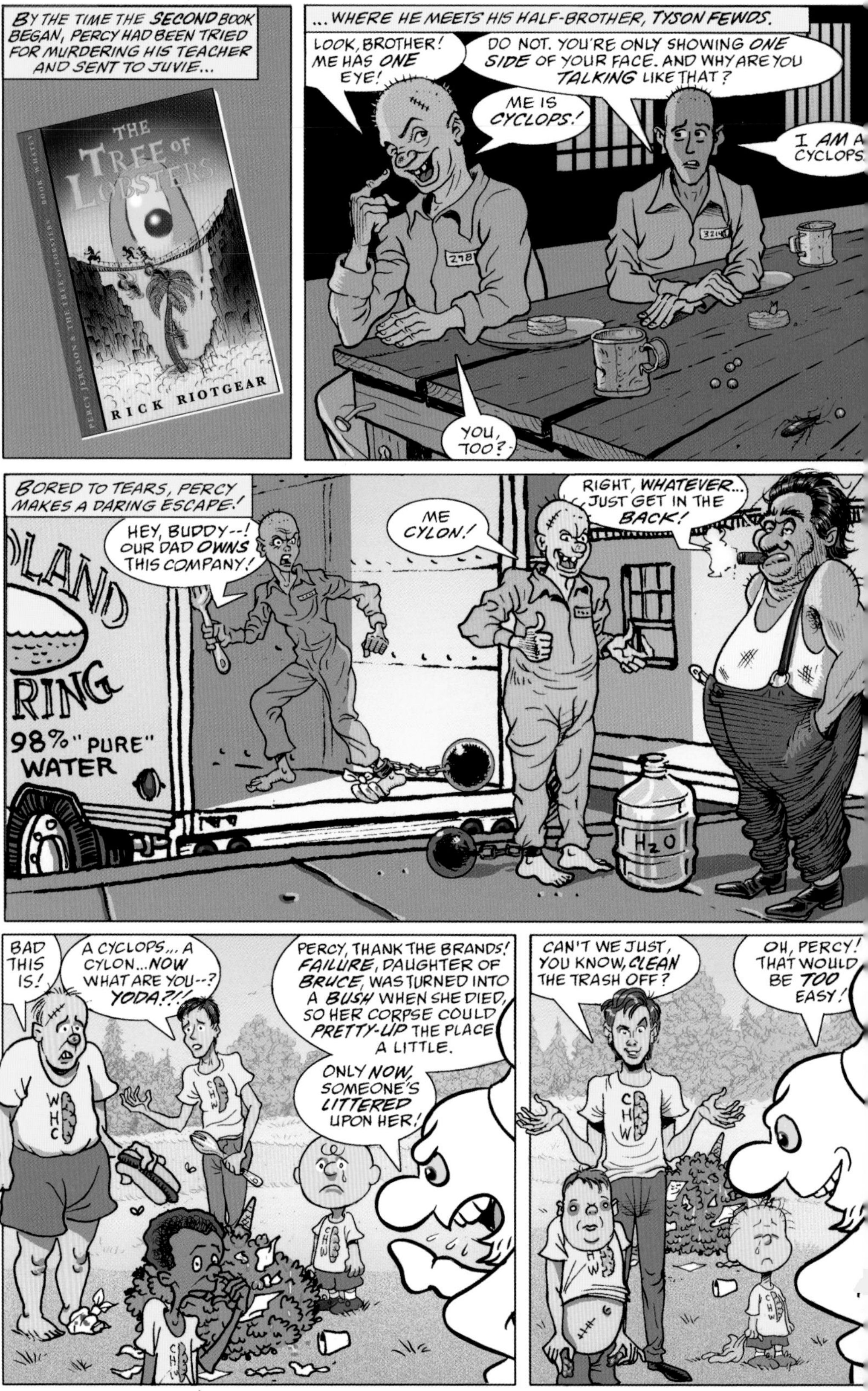

BY THE TIME THE SECOND BOOK BEGAN, PERCY HAD BEEN TRIED FOR MURDERING HIS TEACHER AND SENT TO JUVIE...
THE TREE OF LOBSTERS
RICK RIOTGEAR
PERCY JERKSON & THE TREE OF LOBSTERS BOOK WHATEV
... WHERE HE MEETS HIS HALF-BROTHER, TYSON FEWDS.
LOOK, BROTHER! ME HAS ONE EYE!
DO NOT. YOU'RE ONLY SHOWING ONE SIDE OF YOUR FACE. AND WHY ARE YOU TALKING LIKE THAT?
ME IS CYCLOPS!
I AM A CYCLOPS.
YOU, TOO?
BORED TO TEARS, PERCY MAKES A DARING ESCAPE!
HEY, BUDDY--! OUR DAD OWNS THIS COMPANY!
ME CYLON!
RIGHT, WHATEVER... JUST GET IN THE BACK!
RING
98% "PURE" WATER
H_2O
BAD THIS IS!
A CYCLOPS... A CYLON... NOW WHAT ARE YOU--? YODA?!!
PERCY, THANK THE BRANDS! FAILURE, DAUGHTER OF BRUCE, WAS TURNED INTO A BUSH WHEN SHE DIED, SO HER CORPSE COULD PRETTY-UP THE PLACE A LITTLE.
ONLY NOW, SOMEONE'S LITTERED UPON HER!
CAN'T WE JUST, YOU KNOW, CLEAN THE TRASH OFF?
OH, PERCY! THAT WOULD BE TOO EASY!

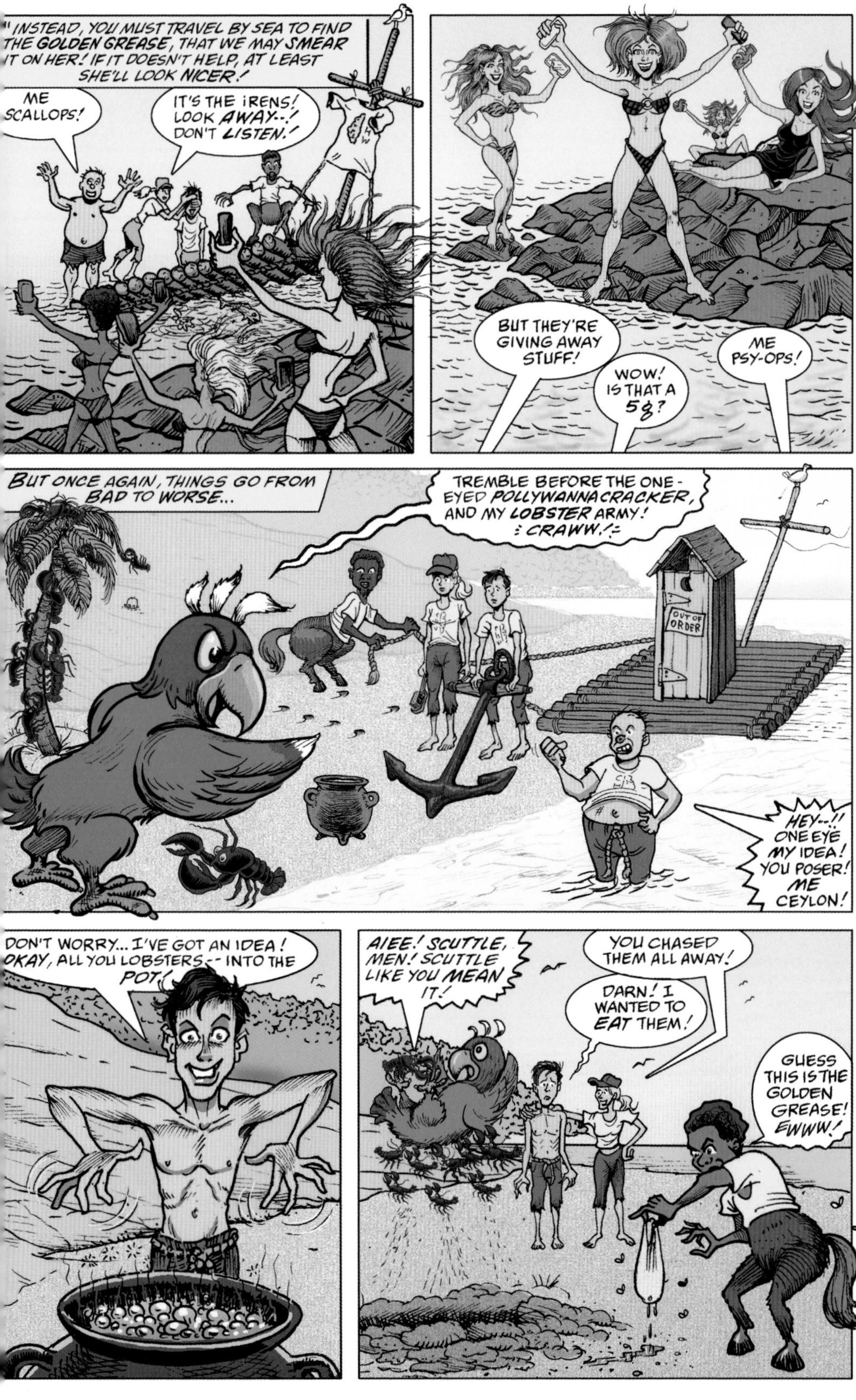
"INSTEAD, YOU MUST TRAVEL BY SEA TO FIND THE GOLDEN GREASE, THAT WE MAY SMEAR IT ON HER! IF IT DOESN'T HELP, AT LEAST SHE'LL LOOK NICER!
ME SCALLOPS!
IT'S THE IRENS! LOOK AWAY--! DON'T LISTEN!
BUT THEY'RE GIVING AWAY STUFF!
WOW! IS THAT A 5G?
ME PSY-OPS!
BUT ONCE AGAIN, THINGS GO FROM BAD TO WORSE...
TREMBLE BEFORE THE ONE-EYED POLLYWANNACRACKER, AND MY LOBSTER ARMY! CRAWW!
OUT OF ORDER
HEY--!! ONE EYE MY IDEA! YOU POSER! ME CEYLON!
DON'T WORRY... I'VE GOT AN IDEA! OKAY, ALL YOU LOBSTERS-- INTO THE POT!
AIEE! SCUTTLE, MEN! SCUTTLE LIKE YOU MEAN IT!
YOU CHASED THEM ALL AWAY!
DARN! I WANTED TO EAT THEM!
GUESS THIS IS THE GOLDEN GREASE! EWWW!

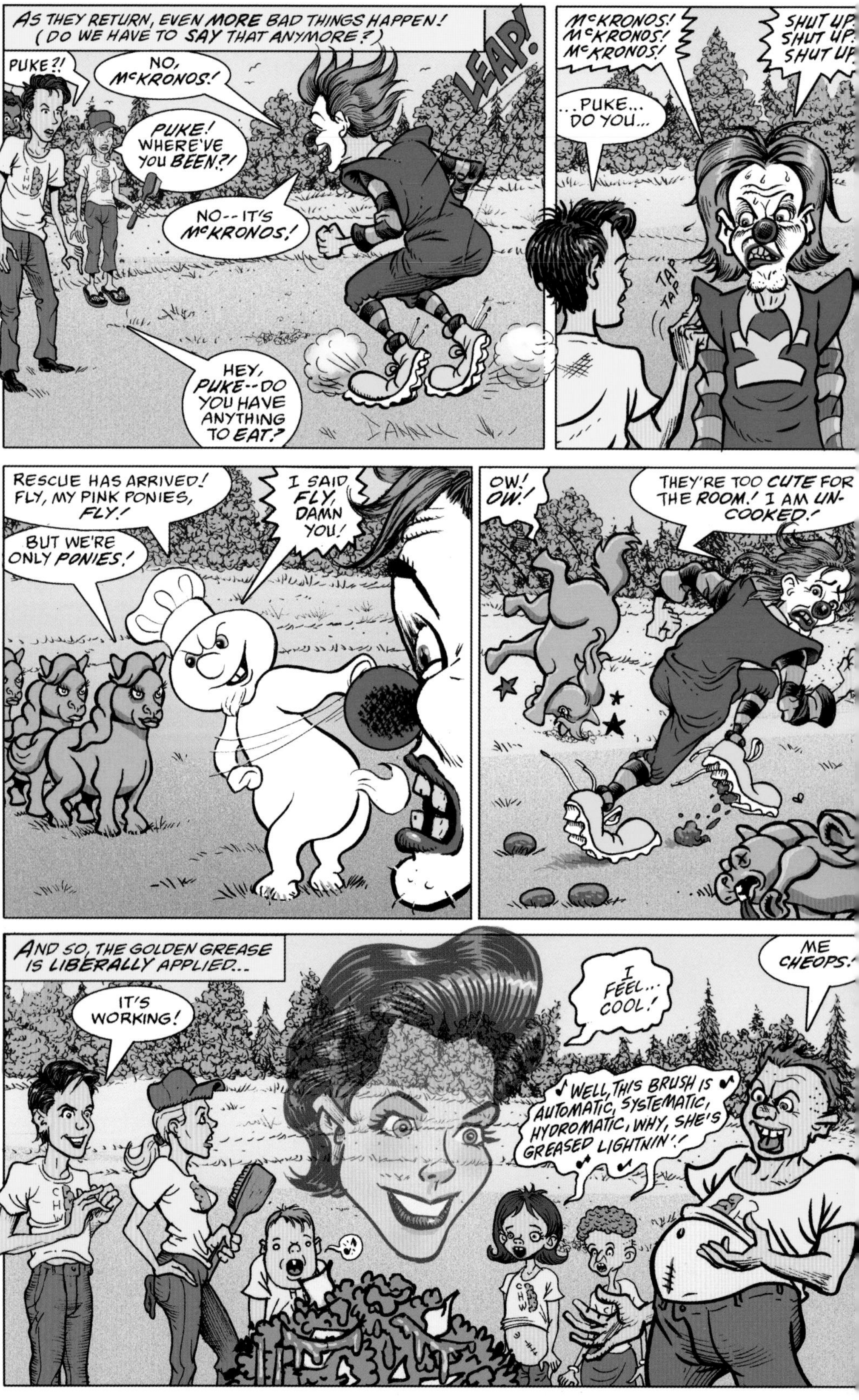
AS THEY RETURN, EVEN MORE BAD THINGS HAPPEN! (DO WE HAVE TO SAY THAT ANYMORE?)
LEAP!
PUKE?!
NO, McKRONOS!
PUKE! WHERE'VE YOU BEEN?!
NO--IT'S McKRONOS!
HEY, PUKE--DO YOU HAVE ANYTHING TO EAT?
McKRONOS! McKRONOS! McKRONOS!
SHUT UP! SHUT UP! SHUT UP!
...PUKE... DO YOU...
TAP TAP
RESCUE HAS ARRIVED! FLY, MY PINK PONIES, FLY!
I SAID FLY, DAMN YOU!
BUT WE'RE ONLY PONIES!
OW! OW!
THEY'RE TOO CUTE FOR THE ROOM! I AM UN-COOKED!
AND SO, THE GOLDEN GREASE IS LIBERALLY APPLIED...
IT'S WORKING!
I FEEL... COOL!
ME CHEOPS!
WELL, THIS BRUSH IS AUTOMATIC, SYSTEMATIC, HYDROMATIC, WHY, SHE'S GREASED LIGHTNIN'!

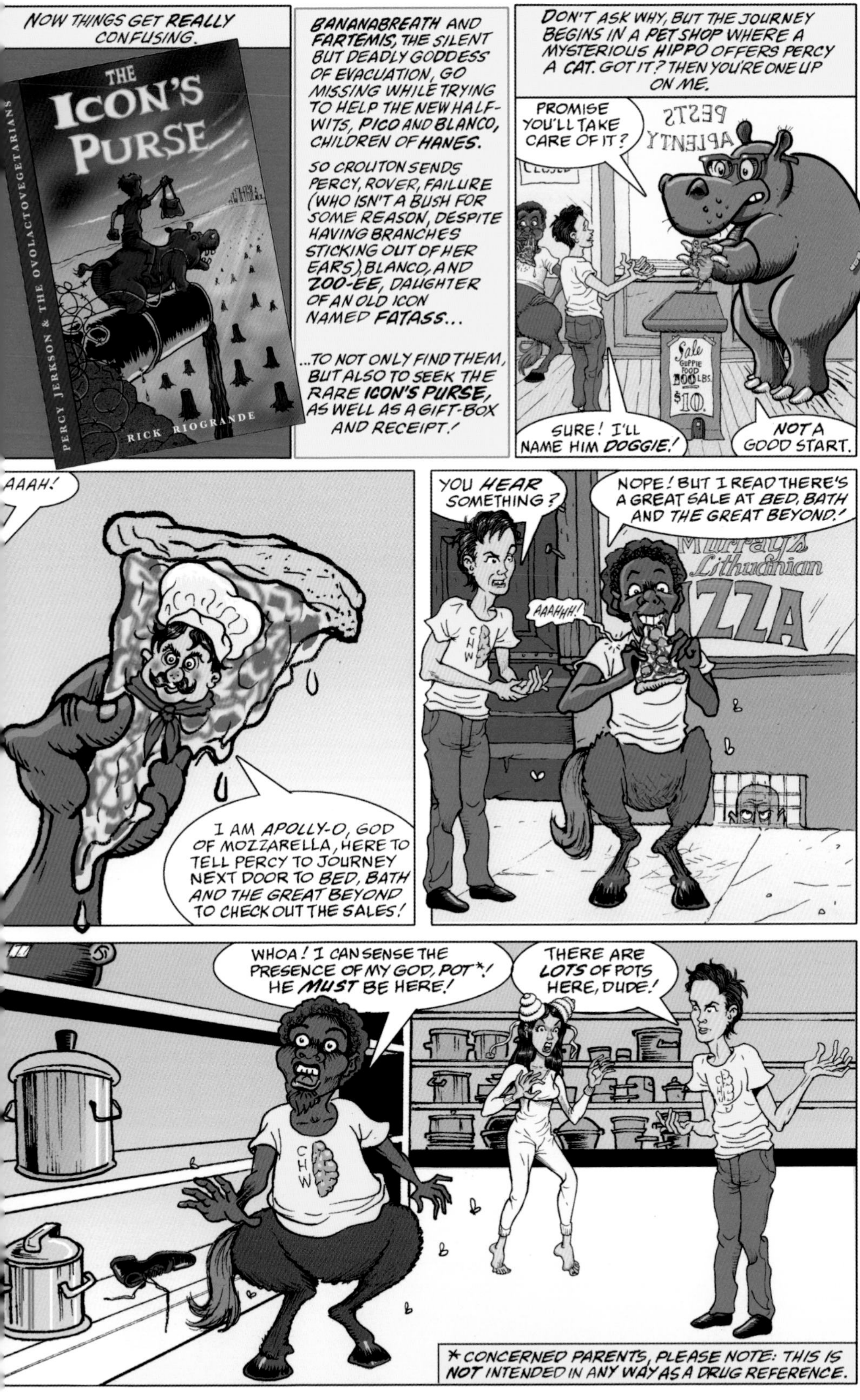
NOW THINGS GET REALLY CONFUSING.
THE ICON'S PURSE
PERCY JERKSON & THE OVOLACTOVEGETARIANS
RICK RIOGRANDE
BANANABREATH AND FARTEMIS, THE SILENT BUT DEADLY GODDESS OF EVACUATION, GO MISSING WHILE TRYING TO HELP THE NEW HALF-WITS, PICO AND BLANCO, CHILDREN OF HANES.
SO CROUTON SENDS PERCY, ROVER, FAILURE (WHO ISN'T A BUSH FOR SOME REASON, DESPITE HAVING BRANCHES STICKING OUT OF HER EARS), BLANCO, AND ZOO-EE, DAUGHTER OF AN OLD ICON NAMED FATASS...
...TO NOT ONLY FIND THEM, BUT ALSO TO SEEK THE RARE ICON'S PURSE, AS WELL AS A GIFT-BOX AND RECEIPT!
DON'T ASK WHY, BUT THE JOURNEY BEGINS IN A PET SHOP WHERE A MYSTERIOUS HIPPO OFFERS PERCY A CAT. GOT IT? THEN YOU'RE ONE UP ON ME.
PROMISE YOU'LL TAKE CARE OF IT?
PESTS APLENTY
Sale GUPPIE FOOD 100 LBS. $10.
SURE! I'LL NAME HIM DOGGIE!
NOT A GOOD START.
AAAH!
I AM APOLLY-O, GOD OF MOZZARELLA, HERE TO TELL PERCY TO JOURNEY NEXT DOOR TO BED, BATH AND THE GREAT BEYOND TO CHECK OUT THE SALES!
YOU HEAR SOMETHING?
NOPE! BUT I READ THERE'S A GREAT SALE AT BED, BATH AND THE GREAT BEYOND!
Murray's Lithuanian ZZA
AAAHH!
WHOA! I CAN SENSE THE PRESENCE OF MY GOD, POT*! HE MUST BE HERE!
THERE ARE LOTS OF POTS HERE, DUDE!
* CONCERNED PARENTS, PLEASE NOTE: THIS IS NOT INTENDED IN ANY WAY AS A DRUG REFERENCE.

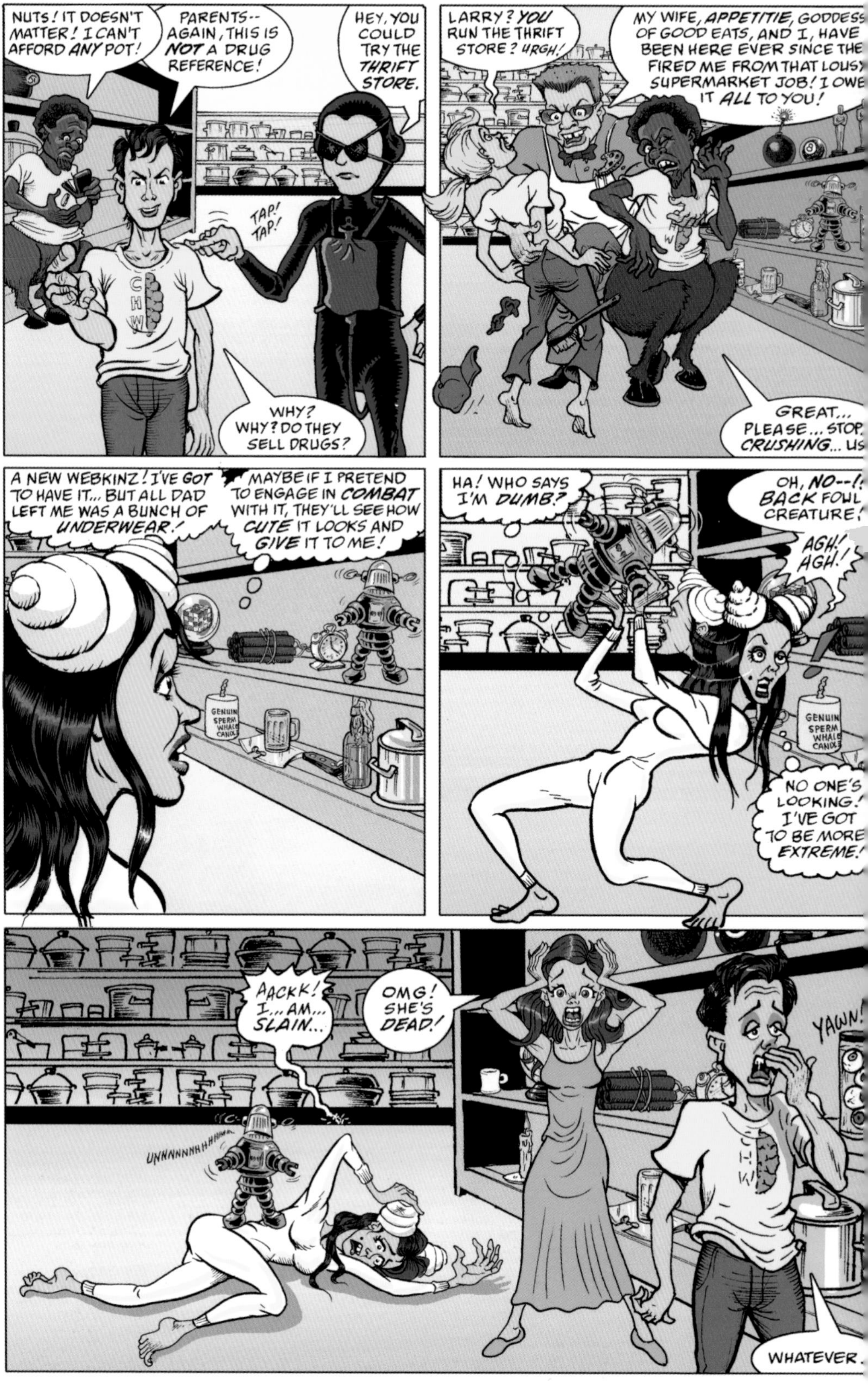
NUTS! IT DOESN'T MATTER! I CAN'T AFFORD ANY POT!
PARENTS-- AGAIN, THIS IS NOT A DRUG REFERENCE!
HEY, YOU COULD TRY THE THRIFT STORE.
CHW
TAP! TAP!
WHY? WHY? DO THEY SELL DRUGS?
LARRY? YOU RUN THE THRIFT STORE? URGH!
MY WIFE, APPETITIE, GODDESS OF GOOD EATS, AND I, HAVE BEEN HERE EVER SINCE THE FIRED ME FROM THAT LOUSY SUPERMARKET JOB! I OWE IT ALL TO YOU!
GREAT... PLEASE... STOP. CRUSHING... US
A NEW WEBKINZ! I'VE GOT TO HAVE IT... BUT ALL DAD LEFT ME WAS A BUNCH OF UNDERWEAR!
MAYBE IF I PRETEND TO ENGAGE IN COMBAT WITH IT, THEY'LL SEE HOW CUTE IT LOOKS AND GIVE IT TO ME!
GENUIN SPERM WHALE CANDL
HA! WHO SAYS I'M DUMB?
OH, NO--! BACK FOUL CREATURE!
AGH! AGH!
GENUIN SPERM WHALE CANDL
NO ONE'S LOOKING! I'VE GOT TO BE MORE EXTREME!
UNNNNNNHHHHH...
AACKK! I... AM... SLAIN...
OMG! SHE'S DEAD!
YAWN!
WHATEVER.

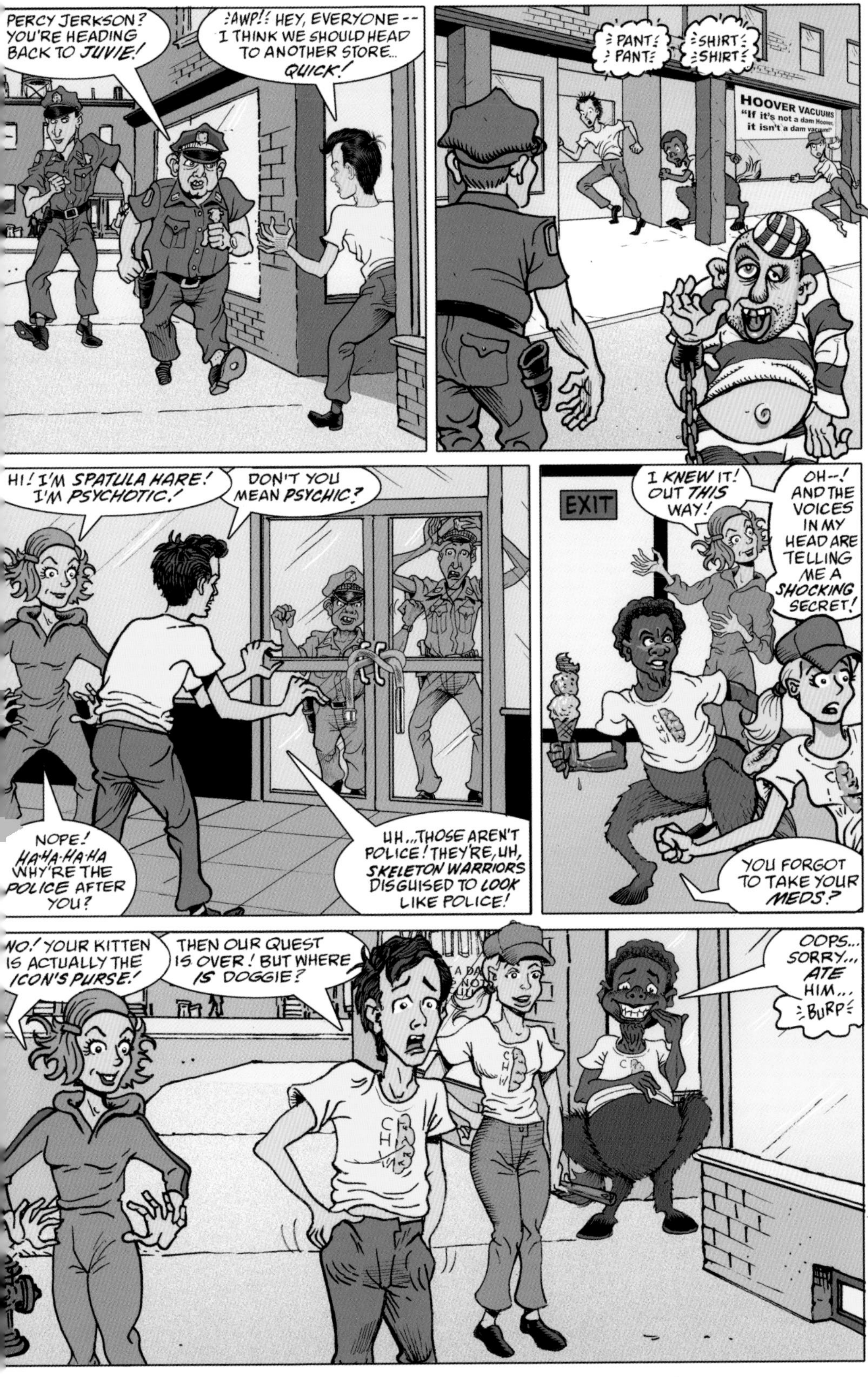

PERCY JERKSON? YOU'RE HEADING BACK TO JUVIE!
AWP!! HEY, EVERYONE -- I THINK WE SHOULD HEAD TO ANOTHER STORE... QUICK!
PANT PANT
SHIRT SHIRT
HOOVER VACUUMS "If it's not a dam Hoover, it isn't a dam vacuum!"
HI! I'M SPATULA HARE! I'M PSYCHOTIC!
DON'T YOU MEAN PSYCHIC?
NOPE! HA-HA-HA-HA WHY'RE THE POLICE AFTER YOU?
UH...THOSE AREN'T POLICE! THEY'RE, UH, SKELETON WARRIORS DISGUISED TO LOOK LIKE POLICE!
EXIT
I KNEW IT! OUT THIS WAY!
OH--! AND THE VOICES IN MY HEAD ARE TELLING ME A SHOCKING SECRET!
YOU FORGOT TO TAKE YOUR MEDS?
NO! YOUR KITTEN IS ACTUALLY THE ICON'S PURSE!
THEN OUR QUEST IS OVER! BUT WHERE IS DOGGIE?
OOPS... SORRY... ATE HIM...
BURP

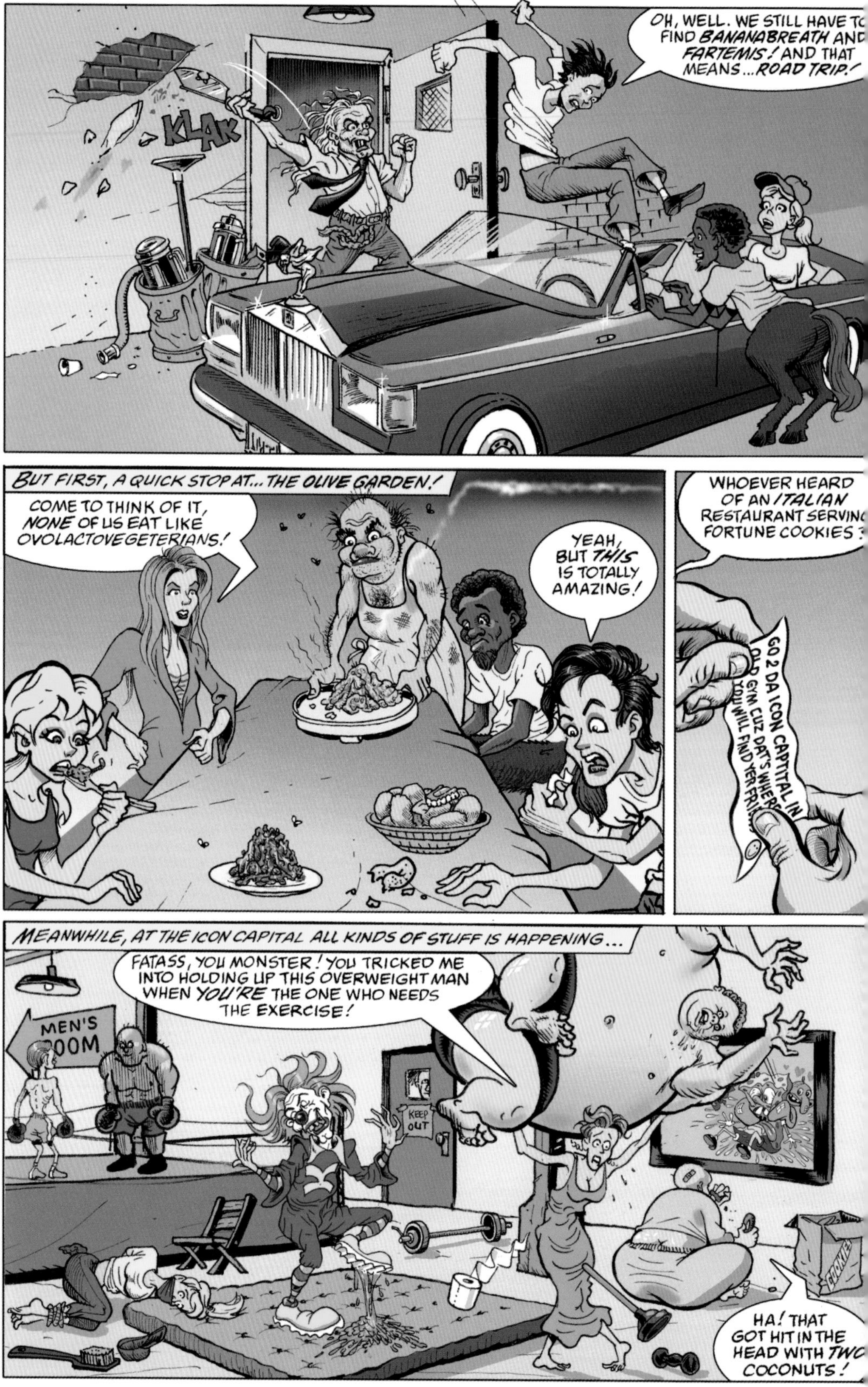
KLAK
OH, WELL. WE STILL HAVE TO FIND *BANANABREATH* AND *FARTEMIS!* AND THAT MEANS... *ROAD TRIP!*
BUT FIRST, A QUICK STOP AT... THE *OLIVE GARDEN!*
COME TO THINK OF IT, *NONE* OF US EAT LIKE OVOLACTOVEGETERIANS!
YEAH, BUT *THIS* IS TOTALLY AMAZING!
WHOEVER HEARD OF AN *ITALIAN* RESTAURANT SERVIN
FORTUNE COOKIES
GO 2 DA ICON CAPITAL IN OLD GYM CUZ DAT'S WHER
YOU WILL FIND YER FRI
MEANWHILE, AT THE ICON CAPITAL ALL KINDS OF STUFF IS HAPPENING...
MEN'S ROOM
FATASS, YOU MONSTER! YOU TRICKED ME INTO HOLDING UP THIS OVERWEIGHT MAN WHEN *YOU'RE* THE ONE WHO NEEDS THE *EXERCISE!*
KEEP OUT
HA! THAT GOT HIT IN THE HEAD WITH *TWO* COCONUTS!

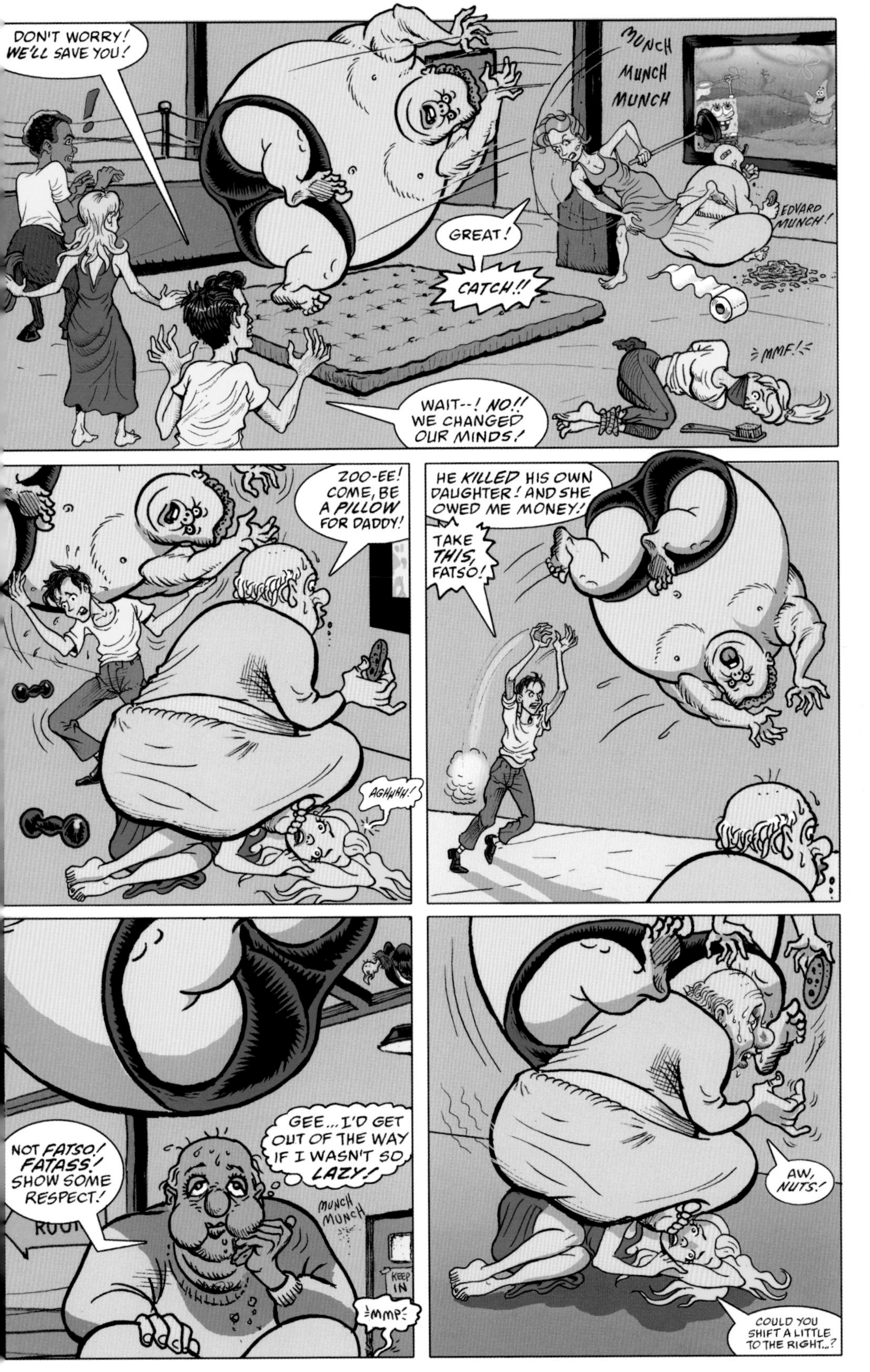
DON'T WORRY! WE'LL SAVE YOU!
!
MUNCH MUNCH MUNCH
EDVARD MUNCH!
GREAT!
CATCH!!
MMF!
WAIT--! NO!! WE CHANGED OUR MINDS!
ZOO-EE! COME, BE A PILLOW FOR DADDY!
AGHHHH!
HE KILLED HIS OWN DAUGHTER! AND SHE OWED ME MONEY!
TAKE THIS, FATSO!
NOT FATSO! FATASS! SHOW SOME RESPECT!
GEE... I'D GET OUT OF THE WAY IF I WASN'T SO LAZY!
MUNCH MUNCH
KEEP IN
MMP!
AW, NUTS!
COULD YOU SHIFT A LITTLE TO THE RIGHT...?

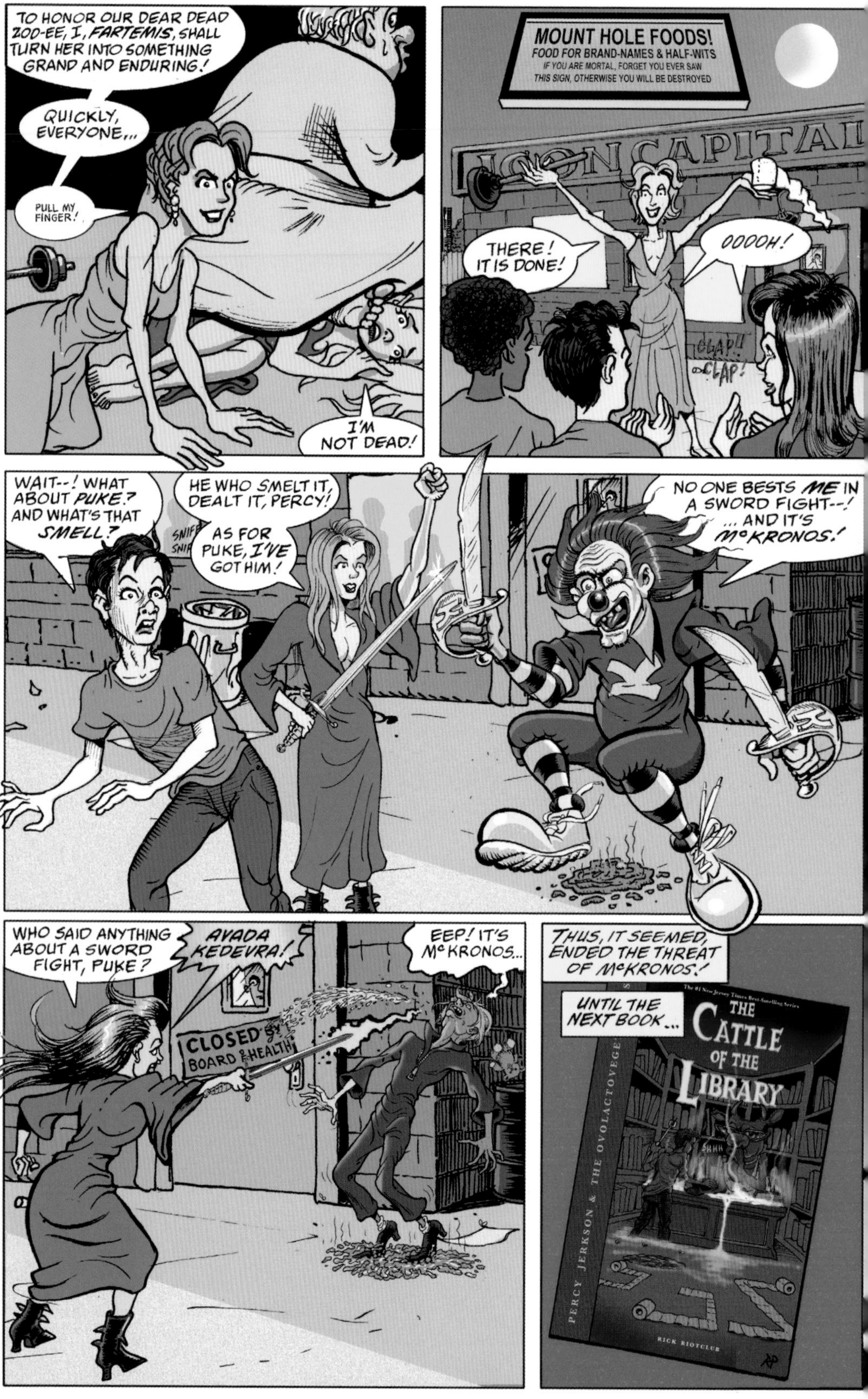
TO HONOR OUR DEAR DEAD ZOO-EE, I, FARTEMIS, SHALL TURN HER INTO SOMETHING GRAND AND ENDURING!
QUICKLY, EVERYONE...
PULL MY FINGER!
I'M NOT DEAD!
MOUNT HOLE FOODS!
FOOD FOR BRAND-NAMES & HALF-WITS
IF YOU ARE MORTAL, FORGET YOU EVER SAW THIS SIGN, OTHERWISE YOU WILL BE DESTROYED
THERE! IT IS DONE!
OOOOH!
CLAP!!
CLAP!
WAIT--! WHAT ABOUT PUKE? AND WHAT'S THAT SMELL?
HE WHO SMELT IT, DEALT IT, PERCY!
AS FOR PUKE, I'VE GOT HIM!
NO ONE BESTS ME IN A SWORD FIGHT--! ... AND IT'S McKRONOS!
WHO SAID ANYTHING ABOUT A SWORD FIGHT, PUKE?
AVADA KEDEVRA!
EEP! IT'S McKRONOS...
CLOSED BY BOARD OF HEALTH
THUS, IT SEEMED, ENDED THE THREAT OF McKRONOS!
UNTIL THE NEXT BOOK...
The #1 New Jersey Times Best-Smelling Series
THE CATTLE OF THE LIBRARY
PERCY JERKSON & THE OVOLACTOVEGE
RICK RIOTCLUB

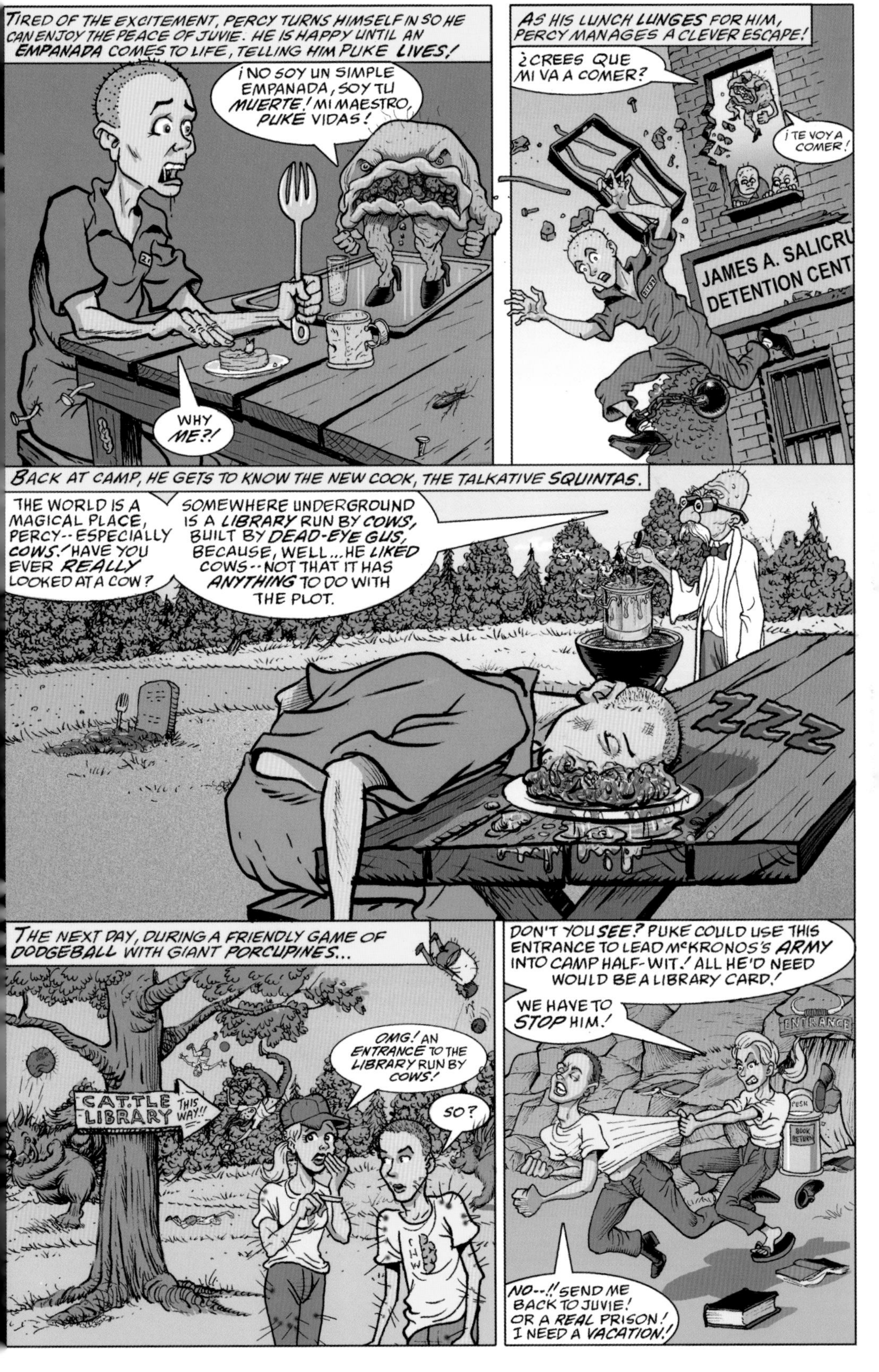
TIRED OF THE EXCITEMENT, PERCY TURNS HIMSELF IN SO HE CAN ENJOY THE PEACE OF JUVIE. HE IS HAPPY UNTIL AN EMPANADA COMES TO LIFE, TELLING HIM PUKE LIVES!
¡NO SOY UN SIMPLE EMPANADA, SOY TU MUERTE! MI MAESTRO, PUKE VIDAS!
WHY ME?!
AS HIS LUNCH LUNGES FOR HIM, PERCY MANAGES A CLEVER ESCAPE!
¿CREES QUE MI VA A COMER?
¡TE VOY A COMER!
JAMES A. SALICRU
DETENTION CENT
BACK AT CAMP, HE GETS TO KNOW THE NEW COOK, THE TALKATIVE SQUINTAS.
THE WORLD IS A MAGICAL PLACE, PERCY--ESPECIALLY COWS! HAVE YOU EVER REALLY LOOKED AT A COW?
SOMEWHERE UNDERGROUND IS A LIBRARY RUN BY COWS, BUILT BY DEAD-EYE GUS, BECAUSE, WELL...HE LIKED COWS--NOT THAT IT HAS ANYTHING TO DO WITH THE PLOT.
ZZZ
THE NEXT DAY, DURING A FRIENDLY GAME OF DODGEBALL WITH GIANT PORCUPINES...
CATTLE LIBRARY
THIS WAY!!
OMG! AN ENTRANCE TO THE LIBRARY RUN BY COWS!
SO?
DON'T YOU SEE? PUKE COULD USE THIS ENTRANCE TO LEAD McKRONOS'S ARMY INTO CAMP HALF-WIT! ALL HE'D NEED WOULD BE A LIBRARY CARD!
WE HAVE TO STOP HIM!
ENTRANCE
PUSH
BOOK RETURN
NO--!! SEND ME BACK TO JUVIE! OR A REAL PRISON! I NEED A VACATION!

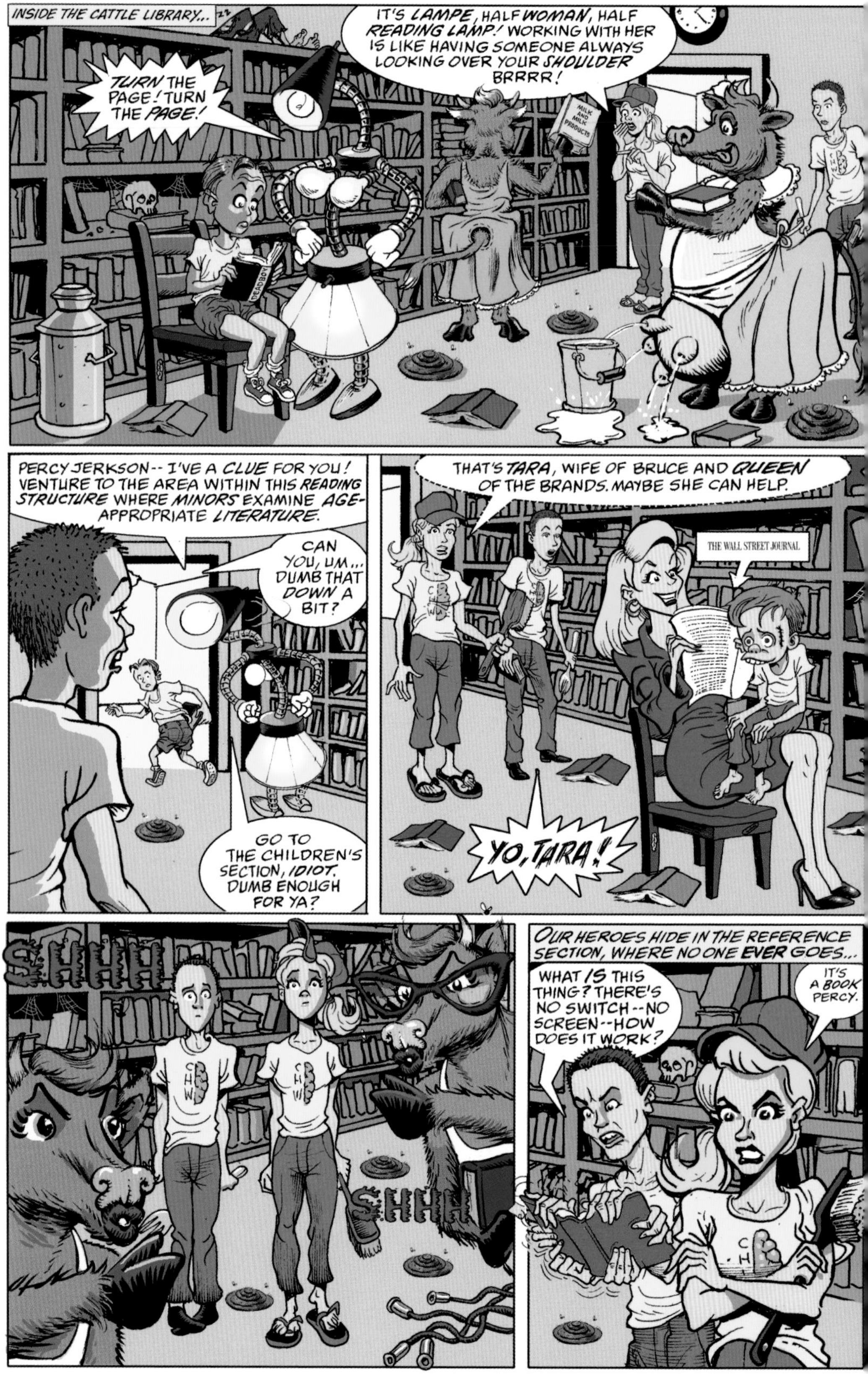
INSIDE THE CATTLE LIBRARY...
IT'S LAMPE, HALF WOMAN, HALF READING LAMP! WORKING WITH HER IS LIKE HAVING SOMEONE ALWAYS LOOKING OVER YOUR SHOULDER BRRRR!
TURN THE PAGE! TURN THE PAGE!
DEADBOY
MILK AND MILK PRODUCTS
PERCY JERKSON-- I'VE A CLUE FOR YOU! VENTURE TO THE AREA WITHIN THIS READING STRUCTURE WHERE MINORS EXAMINE AGE-APPROPRIATE LITERATURE.
CAN YOU, UM... DUMB THAT DOWN A BIT?
GO TO THE CHILDREN'S SECTION, IDIOT. DUMB ENOUGH FOR YA?
THAT'S TARA, WIFE OF BRUCE AND QUEEN OF THE BRANDS. MAYBE SHE CAN HELP.
THE WALL STREET JOURNAL
YO, TARA!
SHHH
SHHH
OUR HEROES HIDE IN THE REFERENCE SECTION, WHERE NO ONE EVER GOES...
WHAT IS THIS THING? THERE'S NO SWITCH--NO SCREEN--HOW DOES IT WORK?
IT'S A BOOK PERCY.

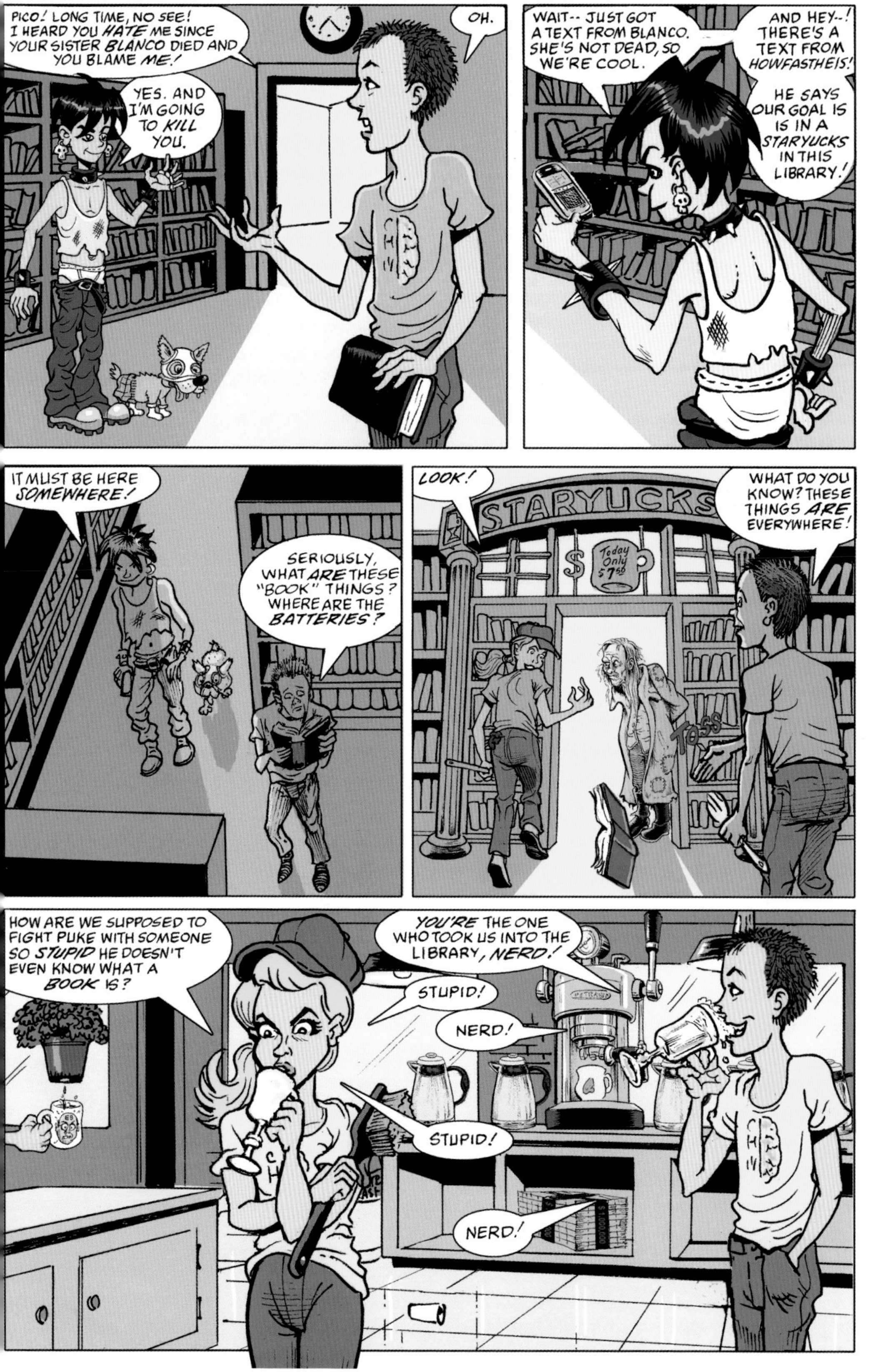
PICO! LONG TIME, NO SEE! I HEARD YOU HATE ME SINCE YOUR SISTER BLANCO DIED AND YOU BLAME ME!
OH.
YES. AND I'M GOING TO KILL YOU.
WAIT-- JUST GOT A TEXT FROM BLANCO. SHE'S NOT DEAD, SO WE'RE COOL.
AND HEY--! THERE'S A TEXT FROM HOWFASTHEIS!
HE SAYS OUR GOAL IS IS IN A STARYUCKS IN THIS LIBRARY!
IT MUST BE HERE SOMEWHERE!
SERIOUSLY, WHAT ARE THESE "BOOK" THINGS? WHERE ARE THE BATTERIES?
LOOK!
STARYUCKS
Today Only $7.50
WHAT DO YOU KNOW? THESE THINGS ARE EVERYWHERE!
TOSS
HOW ARE WE SUPPOSED TO FIGHT PUKE WITH SOMEONE SO STUPID HE DOESN'T EVEN KNOW WHAT A BOOK IS?
YOU'RE THE ONE WHO TOOK US INTO THE LIBRARY, NERD!
STUPID!
NERD!
STUPID!
NERD!

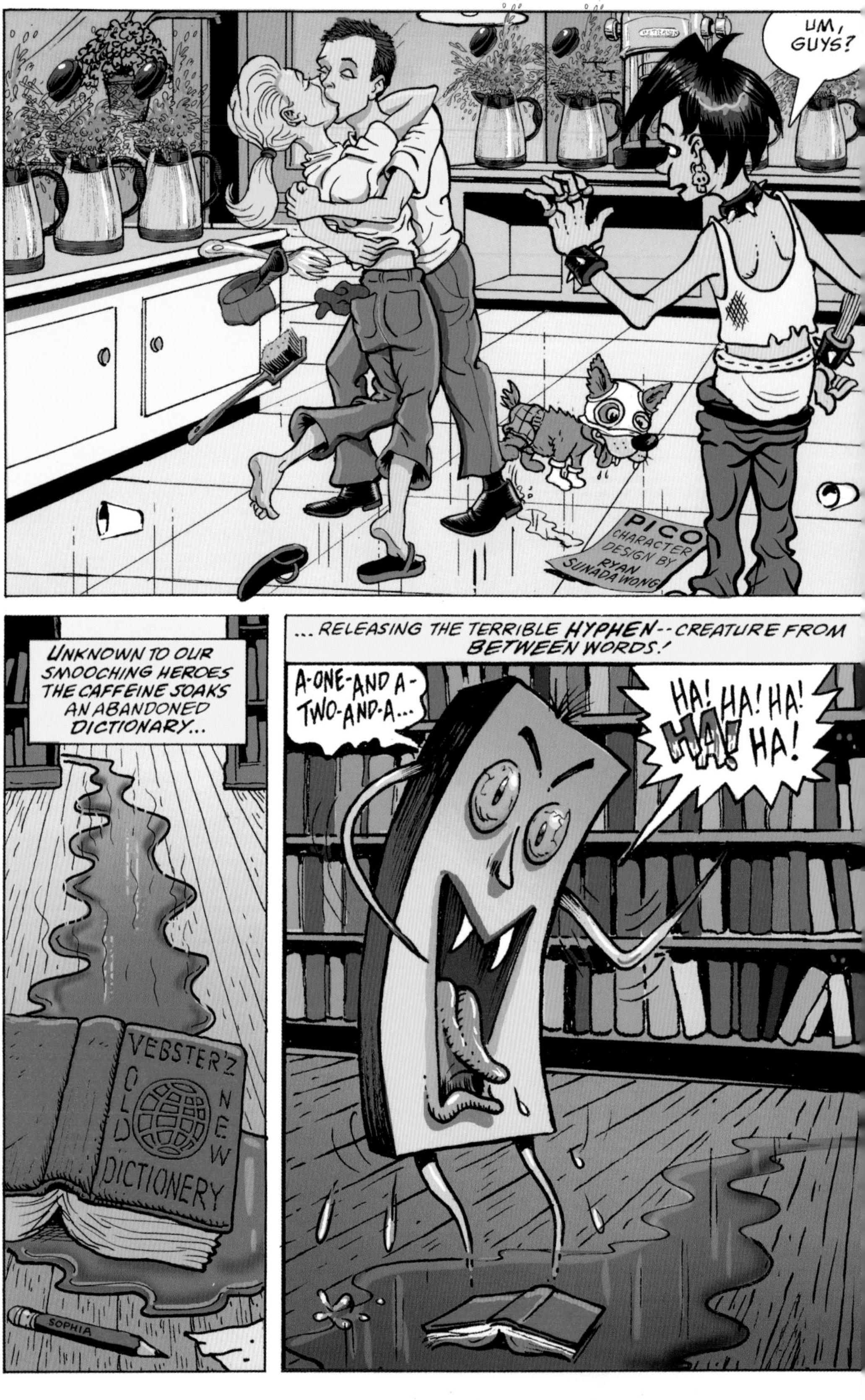
UM, GUYS?
PICO CHARACTER DESIGN BY RYAN SUNADA WONG
UNKNOWN TO OUR SMOOCHING HEROES THE CAFFEINE SOAKS AN ABANDONED DICTIONARY...
VEBSTER'Z OLD NEW DICTIONERY
SOPHIA
... RELEASING THE TERRIBLE HYPHEN--CREATURE FROM BETWEEN WORDS!
A-ONE-AND A-TWO-AND-A...
HA! HA! HA! HA! HA!

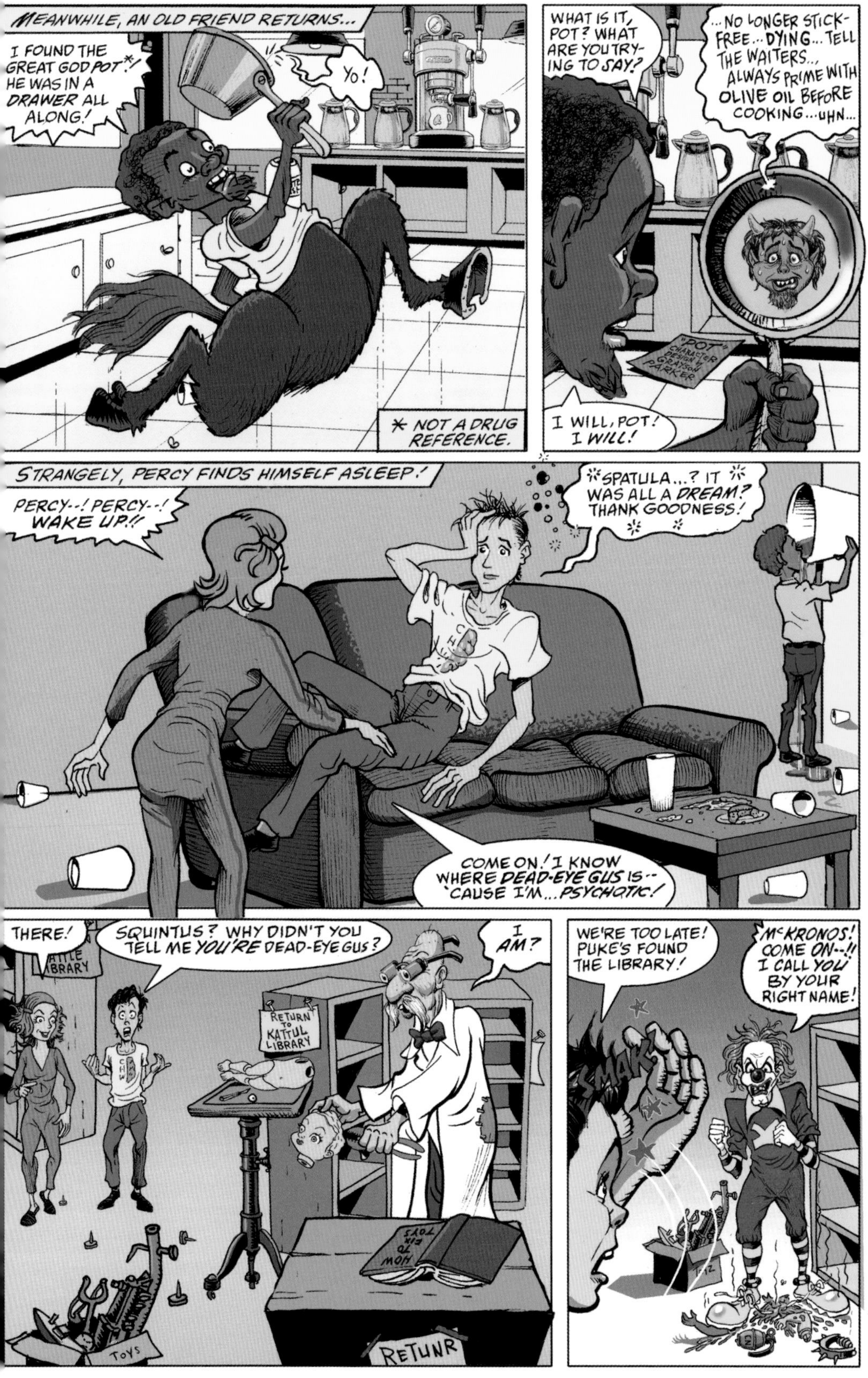

MEANWHILE, AN OLD FRIEND RETURNS...
I FOUND THE GREAT GOD POT*! HE WAS IN A DRAWER ALL ALONG!
YO!
* NOT A DRUG REFERENCE.
WHAT IS IT, POT? WHAT ARE YOU TRYING TO SAY?
...NO LONGER STICK-FREE... DYING... TELL THE WAITERS... ALWAYS PRIME WITH OLIVE OIL BEFORE COOKING...UHN...
"POT" CHARACTER DESIGN by GRAYSON PARKER
I WILL, POT! I WILL!
STRANGELY, PERCY FINDS HIMSELF ASLEEP!
PERCY--! PERCY--! WAKE UP!!
SPATULA...? IT WAS ALL A DREAM? THANK GOODNESS!
COME ON! I KNOW WHERE DEAD-EYE GUS IS--'CAUSE I'M... PSYCHOTIC!
THERE!
SQUINTUS? WHY DIDN'T YOU TELL ME YOU'RE DEAD-EYE GUS?
I AM?
RETURN TO KATTUL LIBRARY
HOW TO FIX TOYS
TOYS
RETUNR
WE'RE TOO LATE! PUKE'S FOUND THE LIBRARY!
McKRONOS! COME ON--!! I CALL YOU BY YOUR RIGHT NAME!
SMAK!

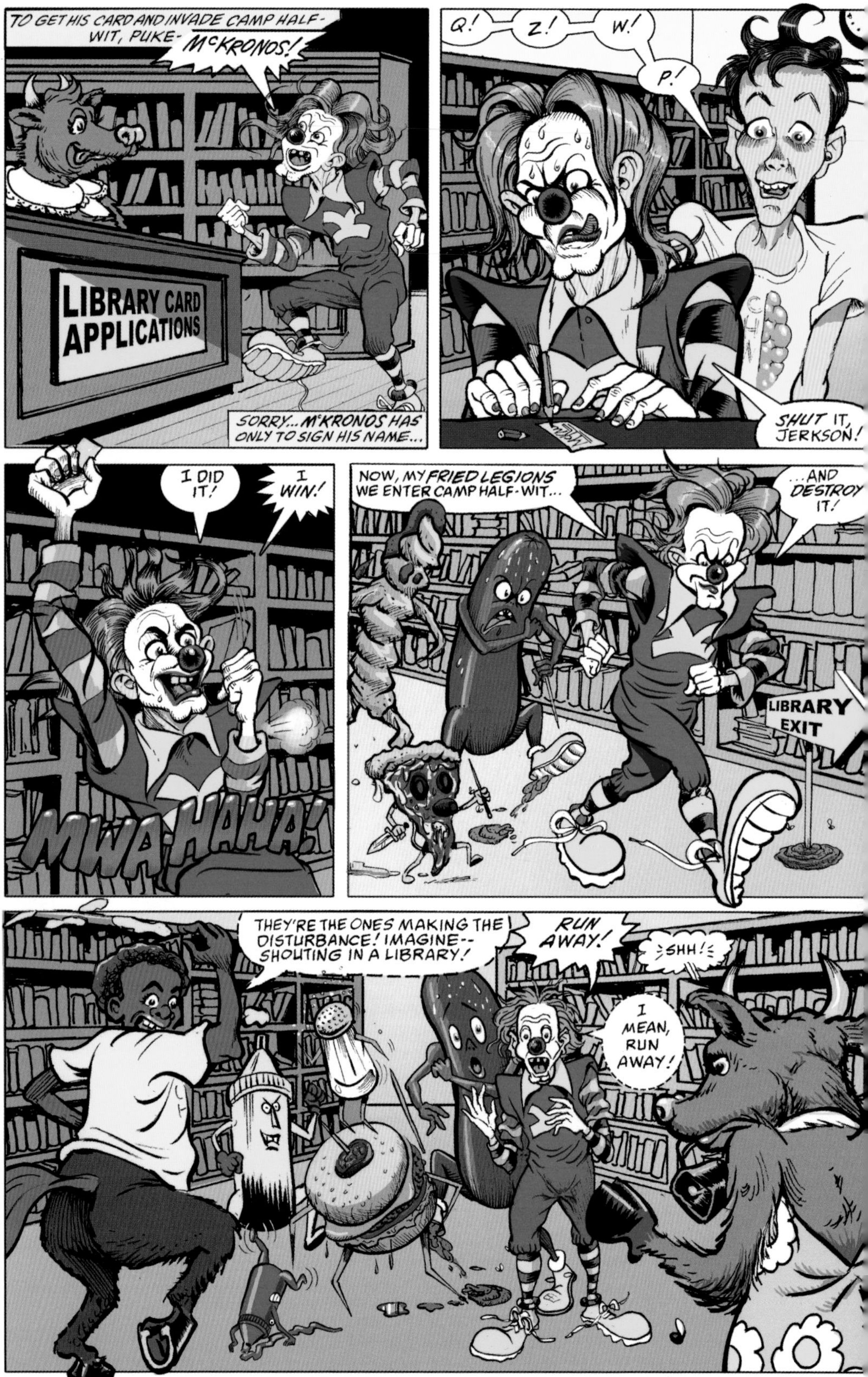

TO GET HIS CARD AND INVADE CAMP HALF-WIT, PUKE-
M^cKRONOS!
LIBRARY CARD APPLICATIONS
SORRY... M^cKRONOS HAS ONLY TO SIGN HIS NAME...
Q!
Z!
W!
P!
SHUT IT, JERKSON!
I DID IT!
I WIN!
MWA-HAHA!
NOW, MY FRIED LEGIONS WE ENTER CAMP HALF-WIT...
...AND DESTROY IT!
LIBRARY EXIT
THEY'RE THE ONES MAKING THE DISTURBANCE! IMAGINE-- SHOUTING IN A LIBRARY!
RUN AWAY!
SHH!
I MEAN, RUN AWAY!

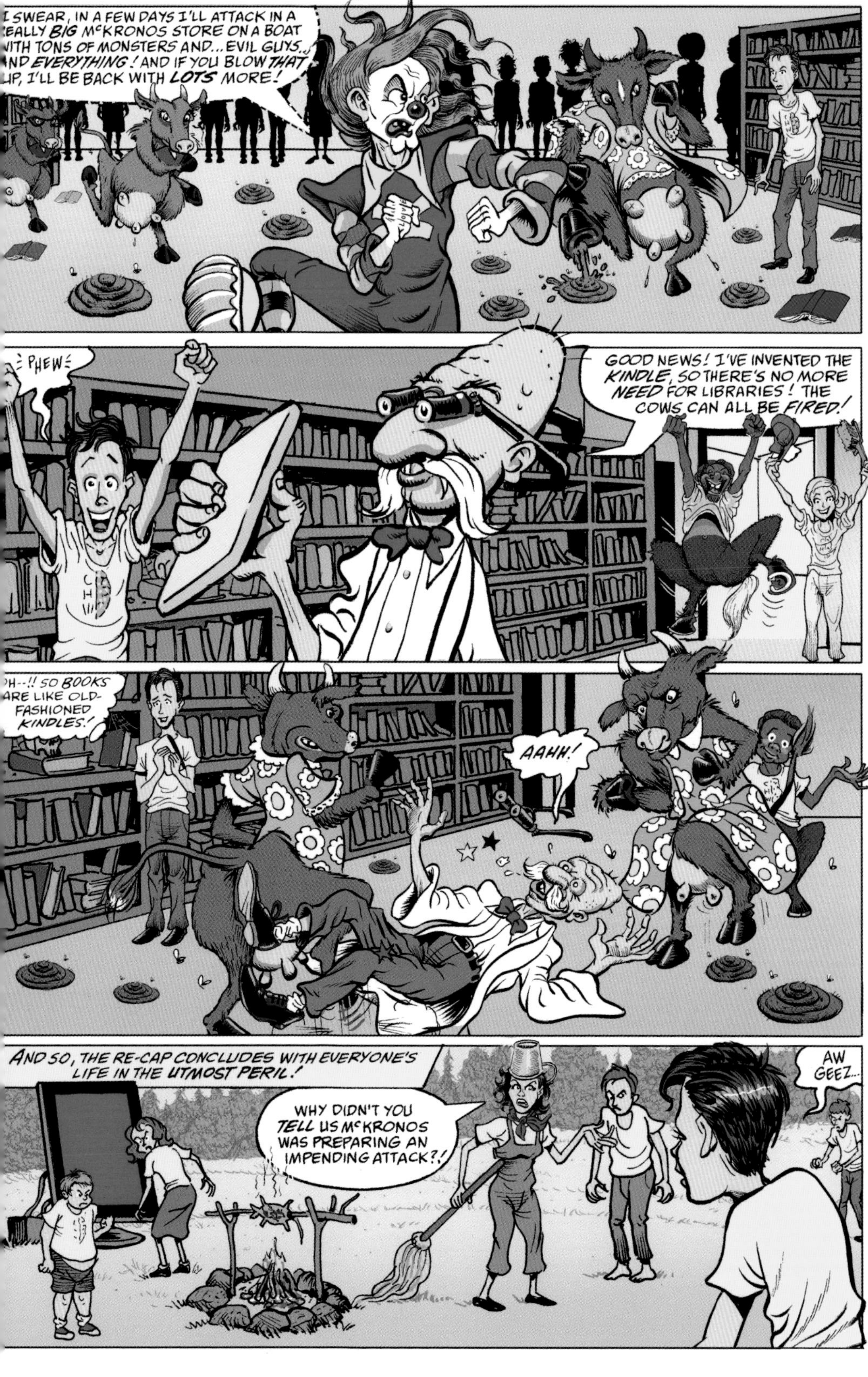
I SWEAR, IN A FEW DAYS I'LL ATTACK IN A REALLY BIG McKRONOS STORE ON A BOAT WITH TONS OF MONSTERS AND... EVIL GUYS... AND EVERYTHING! AND IF YOU BLOW THAT UP, I'LL BE BACK WITH LOTS MORE!
PHEW
GOOD NEWS! I'VE INVENTED THE KINDLE, SO THERE'S NO MORE NEED FOR LIBRARIES! THE COWS CAN ALL BE FIRED!
OH--!! SO BOOKS ARE LIKE OLD-FASHIONED KINDLES!
AAHH!
AND SO, THE RE-CAP CONCLUDES WITH EVERYONE'S LIFE IN THE UTMOST PERIL!
AW GEEZ...
WHY DIDN'T YOU TELL US McKRONOS WAS PREPARING AN IMPENDING ATTACK?!

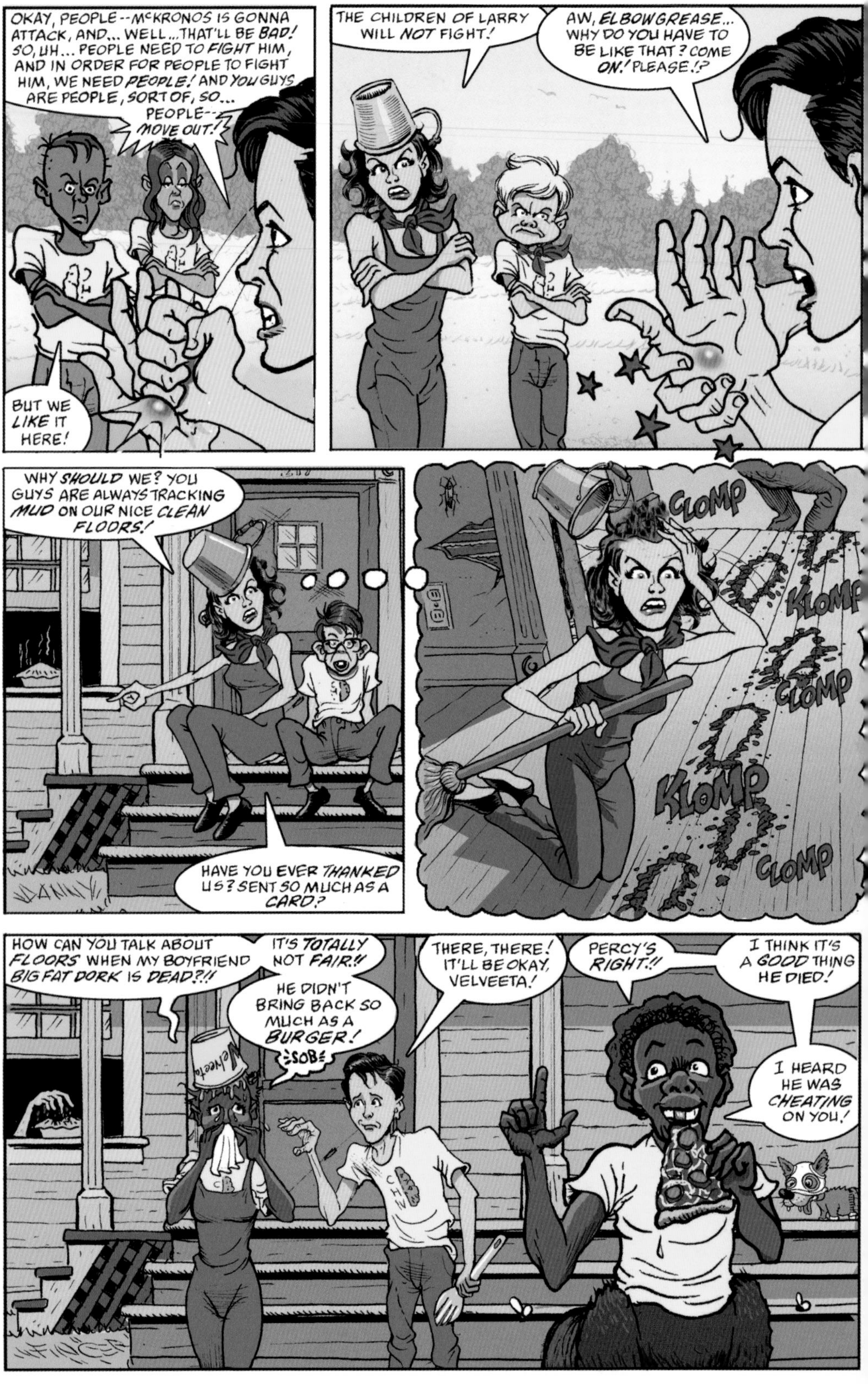

OKAY, PEOPLE--McKRONOS IS GONNA ATTACK, AND... WELL... THAT'LL BE BAD! SO, UH... PEOPLE NEED TO FIGHT HIM, AND IN ORDER FOR PEOPLE TO FIGHT HIM, WE NEED PEOPLE! AND YOU GUYS ARE PEOPLE, SORT OF, SO...
PEOPLE-- MOVE OUT!
BUT WE LIKE IT HERE!
THE CHILDREN OF LARRY WILL NOT FIGHT!
AW, ELBOWGREASE... WHY DO YOU HAVE TO BE LIKE THAT? COME ON! PLEASE!?
WHY SHOULD WE? YOU GUYS ARE ALWAYS TRACKING MUD ON OUR NICE CLEAN FLOORS!
HAVE YOU EVER THANKED US? SENT SO MUCH AS A CARD?
CLOMP
KLOMP
CLOMP
KLOMP
CLOMP
HOW CAN YOU TALK ABOUT FLOORS WHEN MY BOYFRIEND BIG FAT DORK IS DEAD?!!
IT'S TOTALLY NOT FAIR!!
HE DIDN'T BRING BACK SO MUCH AS A BURGER!
SOB
THERE, THERE! IT'LL BE OKAY, VELVEETA!
PERCY'S RIGHT!!
I THINK IT'S A GOOD THING HE DIED!
I HEARD HE WAS CHEATING ON YOU!

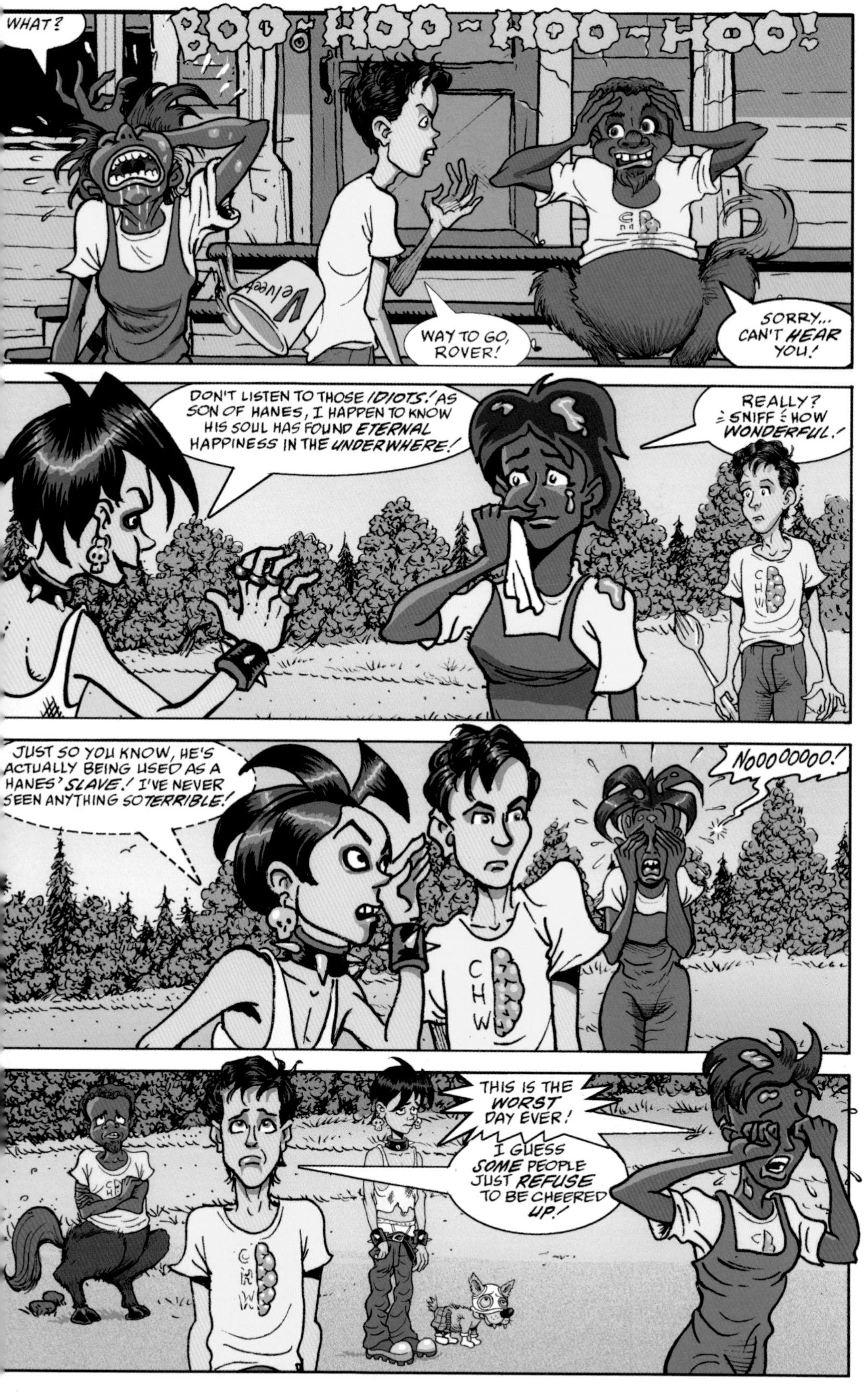
WHAT?
BOO-HOO-HOO-HOO!
WAY TO GO, ROVER!
SORRY... CAN'T HEAR YOU!
DON'T LISTEN TO THOSE IDIOTS! AS SON OF HANES, I HAPPEN TO KNOW HIS SOUL HAS FOUND ETERNAL HAPPINESS IN THE UNDERWHERE!
REALLY? SNIFF HOW WONDERFUL!
JUST SO YOU KNOW, HE'S ACTUALLY BEING USED AS A HANES' SLAVE! I'VE NEVER SEEN ANYTHING SO TERRIBLE!
NOOOOOOOO!
THIS IS THE WORST DAY EVER!
I GUESS SOME PEOPLE JUST REFUSE TO BE CHEERED UP!

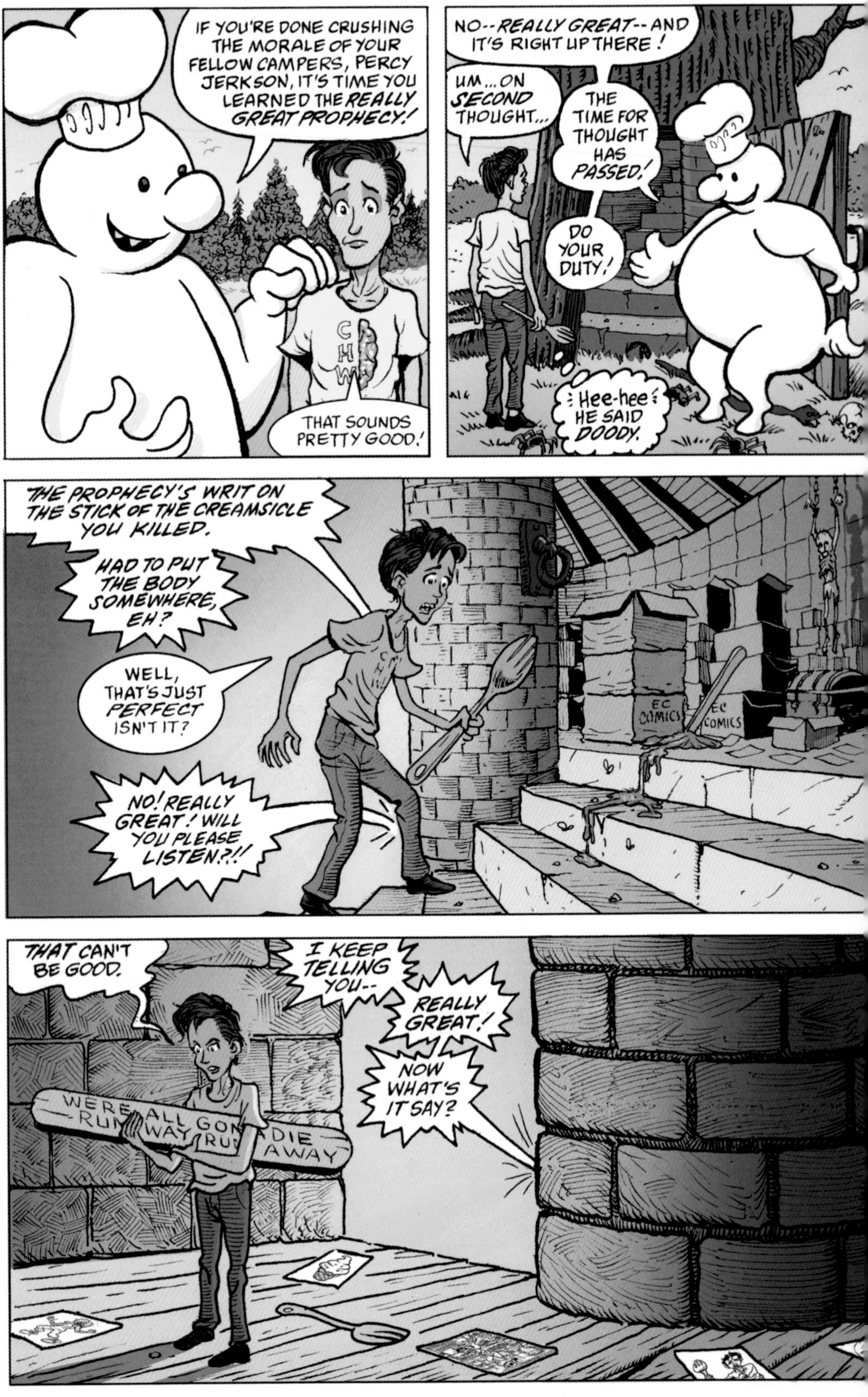
IF YOU'RE DONE CRUSHING THE MORALE OF YOUR FELLOW CAMPERS, PERCY JERKSON, IT'S TIME YOU LEARNED THE REALLY GREAT PROPHECY!
THAT SOUNDS PRETTY GOOD!
NO--REALLY GREAT--AND IT'S RIGHT UP THERE!
UM...ON SECOND THOUGHT...
THE TIME FOR THOUGHT HAS PASSED!
DO YOUR DUTY!
Hee-hee HE SAID DOODY.
THE PROPHECY'S WRIT ON THE STICK OF THE CREAMSICLE YOU KILLED.
HAD TO PUT THE BODY SOMEWHERE, EH?
WELL, THAT'S JUST PERFECT ISN'T IT?
NO! REALLY GREAT! WILL YOU PLEASE LISTEN?!!
EC COMICS
EC COMICS
THAT CAN'T BE GOOD.
I KEEP TELLING YOU--
REALLY GREAT!
NOW WHAT'S IT SAY?
WERE ALL GONNA DIE RUN AWAY RUN AWAY

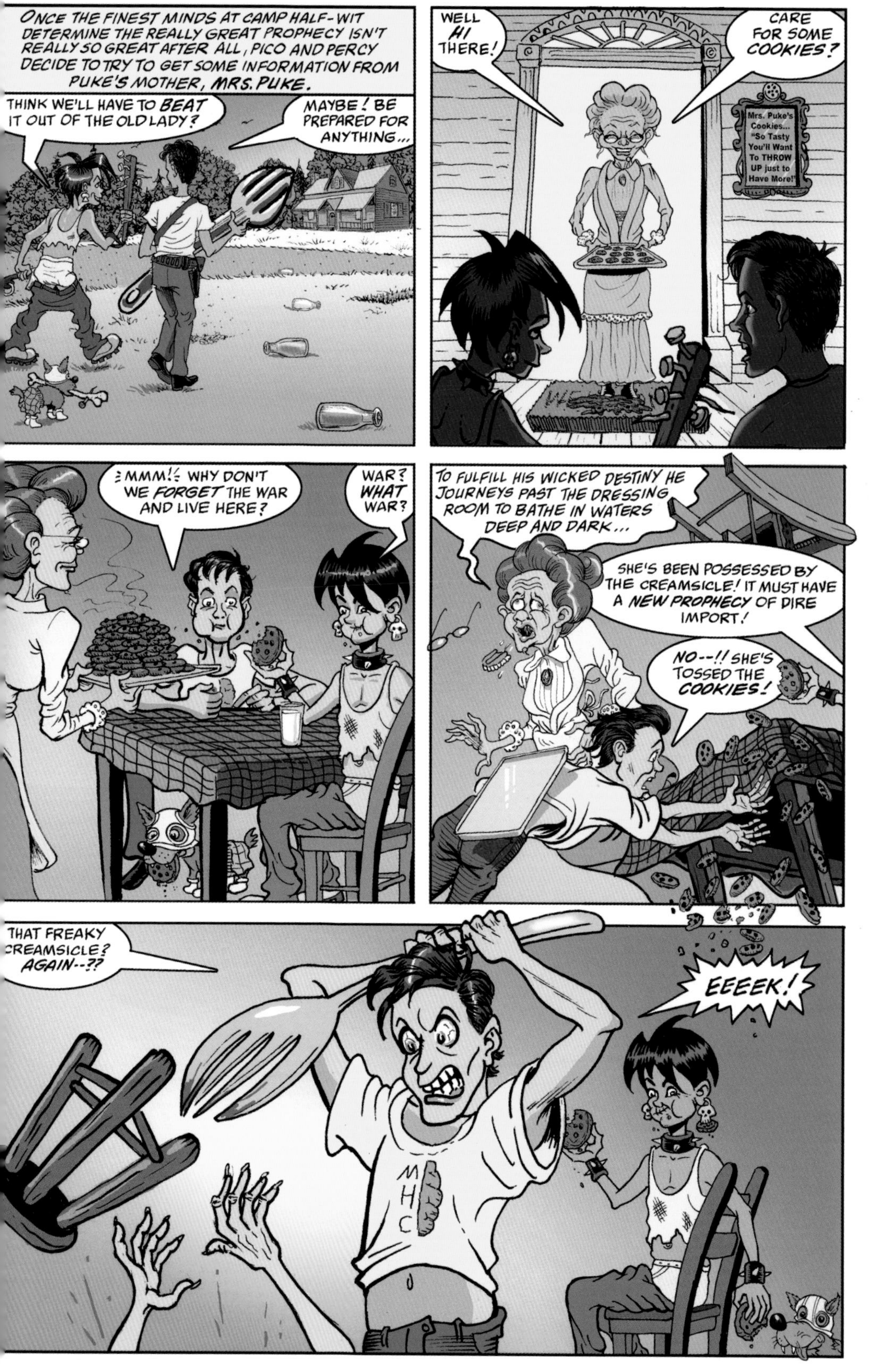
ONCE THE FINEST MINDS AT CAMP HALF-WIT DETERMINE THE REALLY GREAT PROPHECY ISN'T REALLY SO GREAT AFTER ALL, PICO AND PERCY DECIDE TO TRY TO GET SOME INFORMATION FROM PUKE'S MOTHER, MRS. PUKE.
THINK WE'LL HAVE TO BEAT IT OUT OF THE OLD LADY?
MAYBE! BE PREPARED FOR ANYTHING...
WELL HI THERE!
CARE FOR SOME COOKIES?
Mrs. Puke's Cookies... "So Tasty You'll Want To THROW UP just to Have More!"
MMM! WHY DON'T WE FORGET THE WAR AND LIVE HERE?
WAR? WHAT WAR?
TO FULFILL HIS WICKED DESTINY HE JOURNEYS PAST THE DRESSING ROOM TO BATHE IN WATERS DEEP AND DARK...
SHE'S BEEN POSSESSED BY THE CREAMSICLE! IT MUST HAVE A NEW PROPHECY OF DIRE IMPORT!
NO--!! SHE'S TOSSED THE COOKIES!
THAT FREAKY CREAMSICLE? AGAIN--??
EEEEK!
MHC

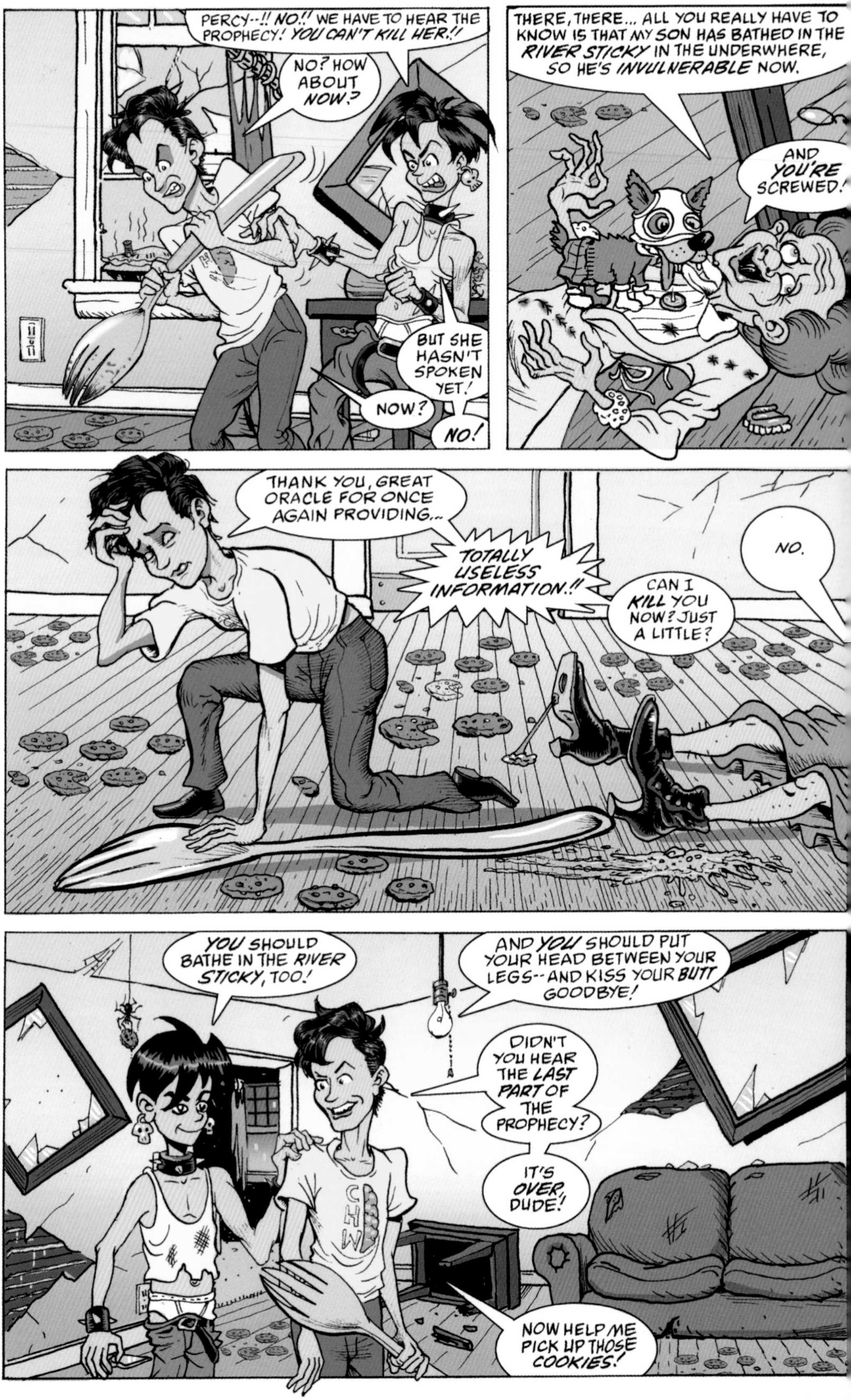
PERCY--!! NO!! WE HAVE TO HEAR THE PROPHECY! YOU CAN'T KILL HER!!
NO? HOW ABOUT NOW?
BUT SHE HASN'T SPOKEN YET!
NOW?
NO!
THERE, THERE... ALL YOU REALLY HAVE TO KNOW IS THAT MY SON HAS BATHED IN THE RIVER STICKY IN THE UNDERWHERE, SO HE'S INVULNERABLE NOW.
AND YOU'RE SCREWED!
THANK YOU, GREAT ORACLE FOR ONCE AGAIN PROVIDING...
TOTALLY USELESS INFORMATION!!
CAN I KILL YOU NOW? JUST A LITTLE?
NO.
YOU SHOULD BATHE IN THE RIVER STICKY, TOO!
AND YOU SHOULD PUT YOUR HEAD BETWEEN YOUR LEGS--AND KISS YOUR BUTT GOODBYE!
DIDN'T YOU HEAR THE LAST PART OF THE PROPHECY?
IT'S OVER, DUDE!
NOW HELP ME PICK UP THOSE COOKIES!

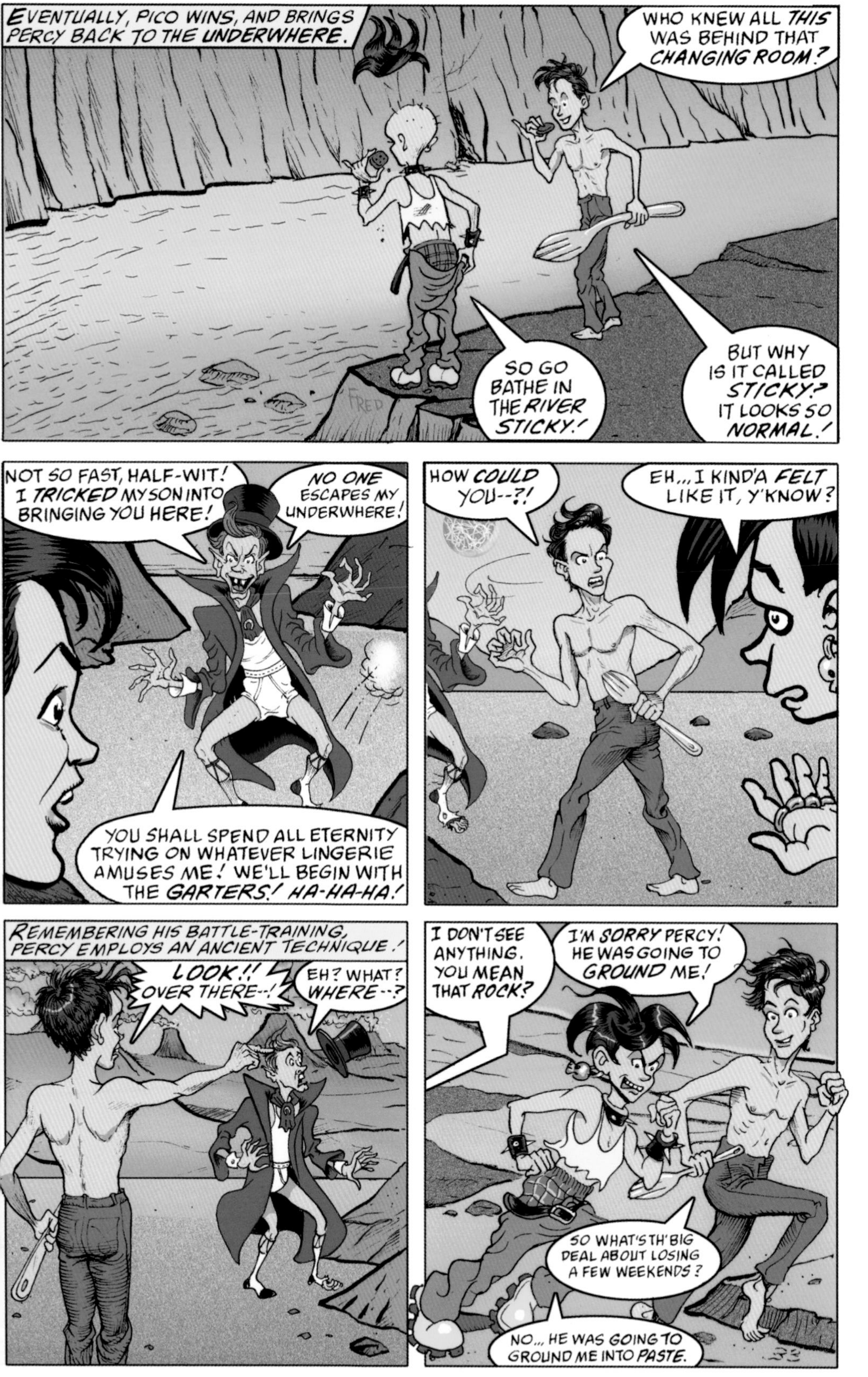

EVENTUALLY, PICO WINS, AND BRINGS PERCY BACK TO THE UNDERWHERE.
WHO KNEW ALL THIS WAS BEHIND THAT CHANGING ROOM?
SO GO BATHE IN THE RIVER STICKY!
BUT WHY IS IT CALLED STICKY? IT LOOKS SO NORMAL!
FRED
NOT SO FAST, HALF-WIT! I TRICKED MY SON INTO BRINGING YOU HERE!
NO ONE ESCAPES MY UNDERWHERE!
YOU SHALL SPEND ALL ETERNITY TRYING ON WHATEVER LINGERIE AMUSES ME! WE'LL BEGIN WITH THE GARTERS! HA-HA-HA!
HOW COULD YOU--?!
EH... I KIND'A FELT LIKE IT, Y'KNOW?
REMEMBERING HIS BATTLE-TRAINING, PERCY EMPLOYS AN ANCIENT TECHNIQUE!
LOOK!! OVER THERE--!
EH? WHAT? WHERE--?
I DON'T SEE ANYTHING. YOU MEAN THAT ROCK?
I'M SORRY PERCY! HE WAS GOING TO GROUND ME!
SO WHAT'S TH' BIG DEAL ABOUT LOSING A FEW WEEKENDS?
NO... HE WAS GOING TO GROUND ME INTO PASTE.

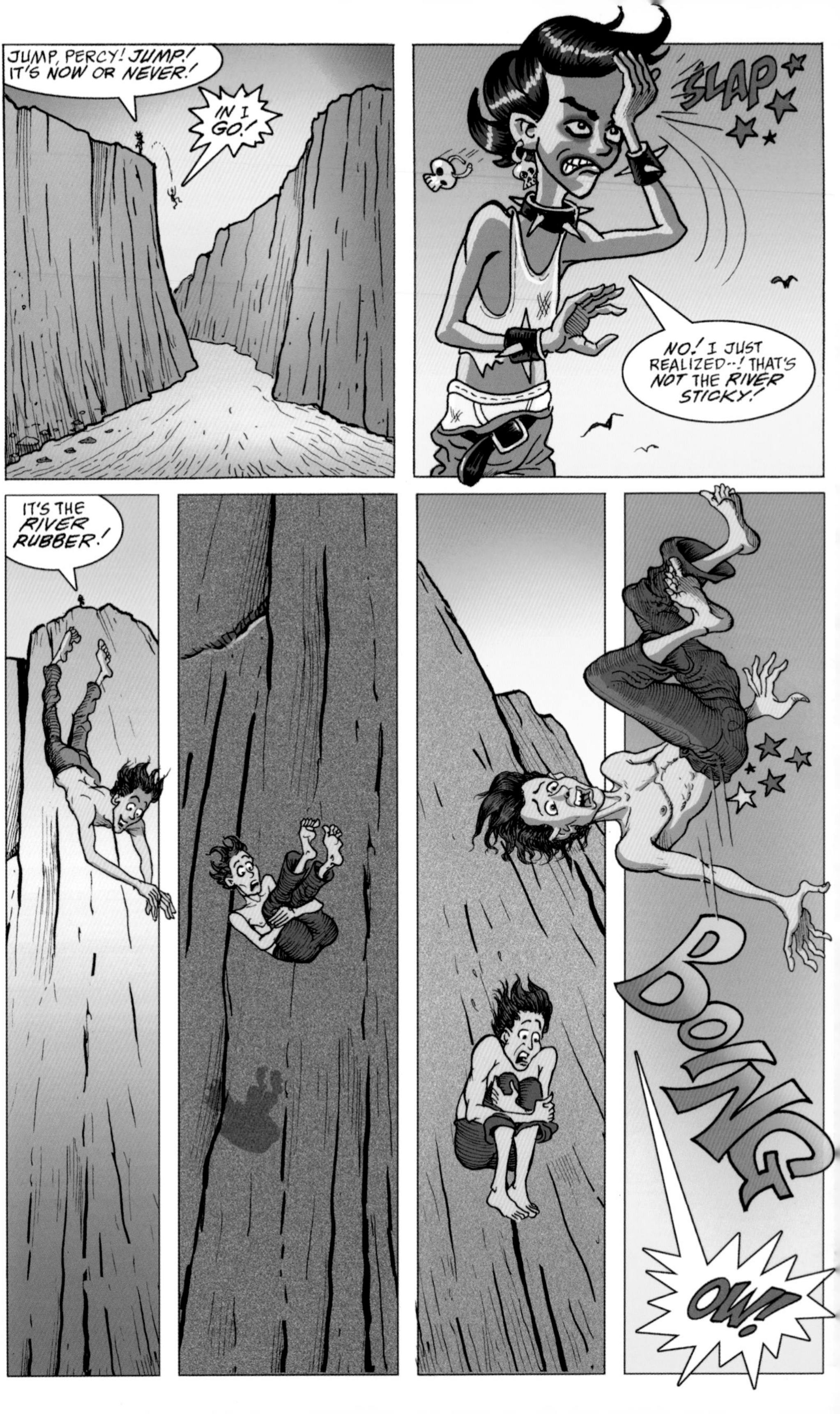
JUMP, PERCY! JUMP! IT'S NOW OR NEVER!
IN I GO!
SLAP
NO! I JUST REALIZED--! THAT'S NOT THE RIVER STICKY!
IT'S THE RIVER RUBBER!
BOING
OW!

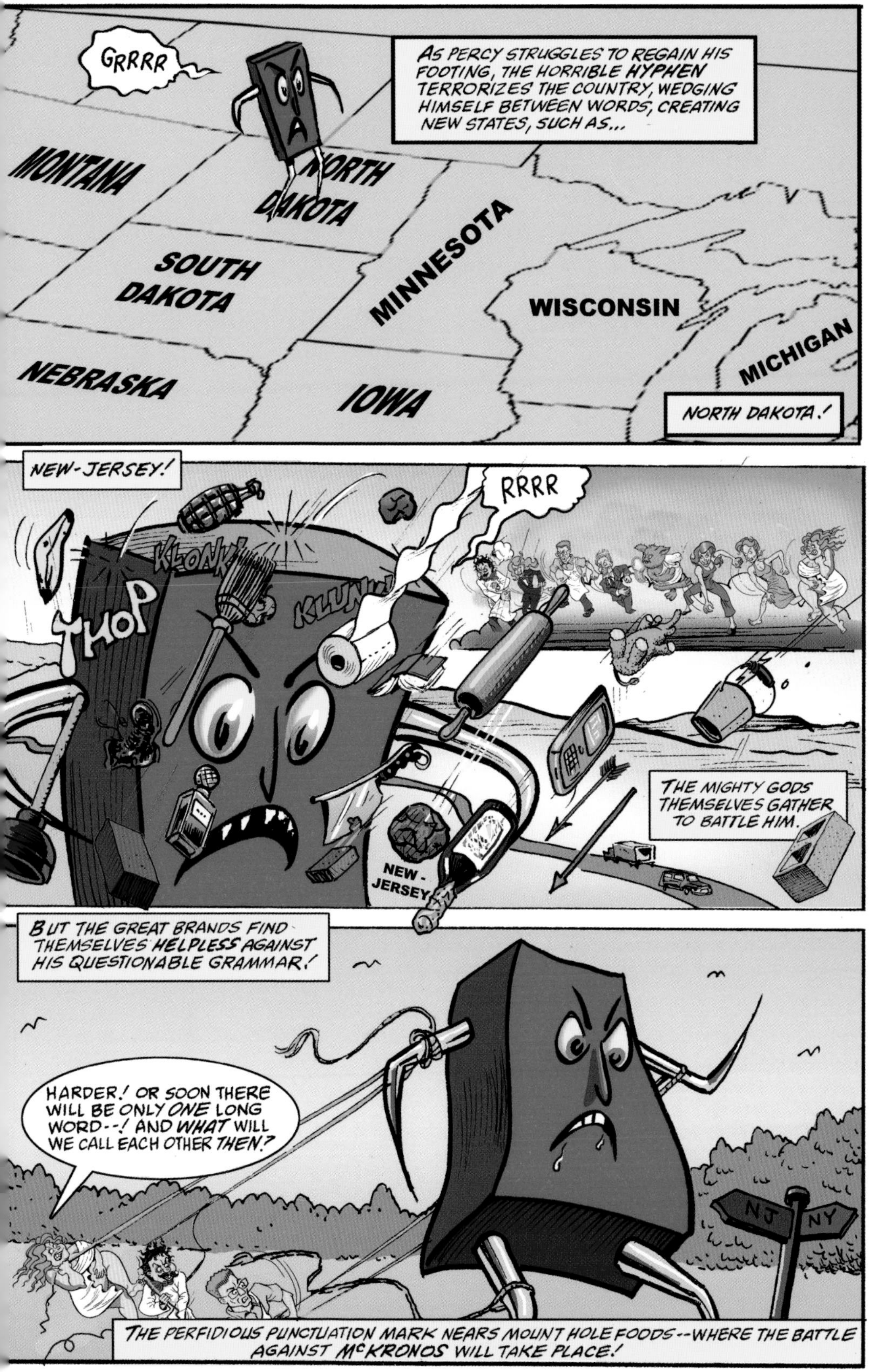
GRRRR
AS PERCY STRUGGLES TO REGAIN HIS FOOTING, THE HORRIBLE HYPHEN TERRORIZES THE COUNTRY, WEDGING HIMSELF BETWEEN WORDS, CREATING NEW STATES, SUCH AS...
MONTANA
NORTH DAKOTA
SOUTH DAKOTA
MINNESOTA
WISCONSIN
MICHIGAN
NEBRASKA
IOWA
NORTH DAKOTA!
NEW-JERSEY!
RRRR
KLONK!
THOP
KLUNK!
NEW - JERSEY
THE MIGHTY GODS THEMSELVES GATHER TO BATTLE HIM.
BUT THE GREAT BRANDS FIND THEMSELVES HELPLESS AGAINST HIS QUESTIONABLE GRAMMAR!
HARDER! OR SOON THERE WILL BE ONLY ONE LONG WORD--! AND WHAT WILL WE CALL EACH OTHER THEN?
NJ
NY
THE PERFIDIOUS PUNCTUATION MARK NEARS MOUNT HOLE FOODS--WHERE THE BATTLE AGAINST McKRONOS WILL TAKE PLACE!

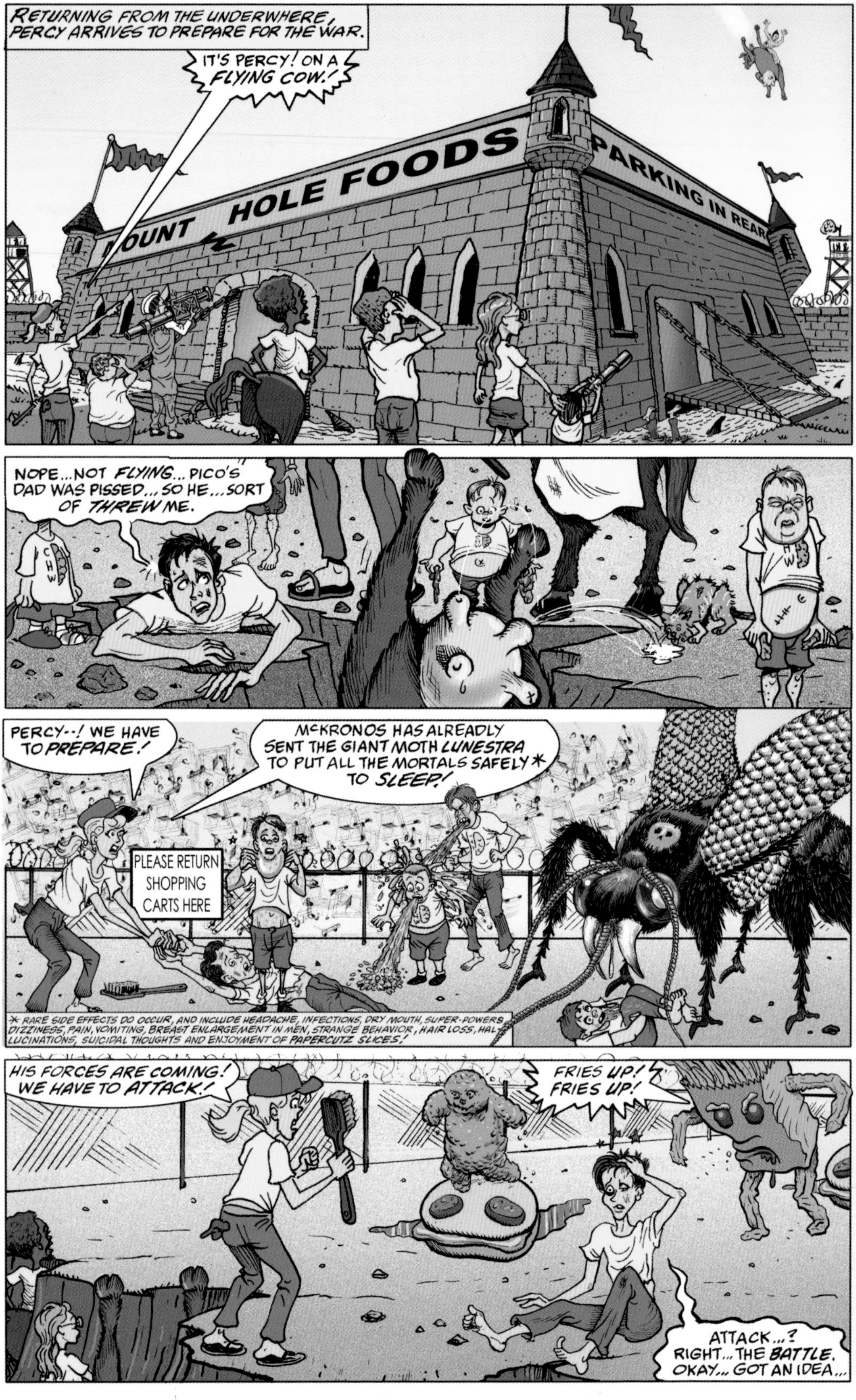
RETURNING FROM THE UNDERWHERE, PERCY ARRIVES TO PREPARE FOR THE WAR.
IT'S PERCY! ON A FLYING COW!
MOUNT HOLE FOODS
PARKING IN REAR
NOPE... NOT FLYING... PICO'S DAD WAS PISSED... SO HE... SORT OF THREW ME.
PERCY--! WE HAVE TO PREPARE!
McKRONOS HAS ALREADY SENT THE GIANT MOTH LUNESTRA TO PUT ALL THE MORTALS SAFELY* TO SLEEP!
PLEASE RETURN SHOPPING CARTS HERE
* RARE SIDE EFFECTS DO OCCUR, AND INCLUDE HEADACHE, INFECTIONS, DRY MOUTH, SUPER-POWERS, DIZZINESS, PAIN, VOMITING, BREAST ENLARGEMENT IN MEN, STRANGE BEHAVIOR, HAIR LOSS, HALLUCINATIONS, SUICIDAL THOUGHTS AND ENJOYMENT OF PAPERCUTZ SLICES!
HIS FORCES ARE COMING! WE HAVE TO ATTACK!
FRIES UP! FRIES UP!
ATTACK...? RIGHT... THE BATTLE. OKAY... GOT AN IDEA...

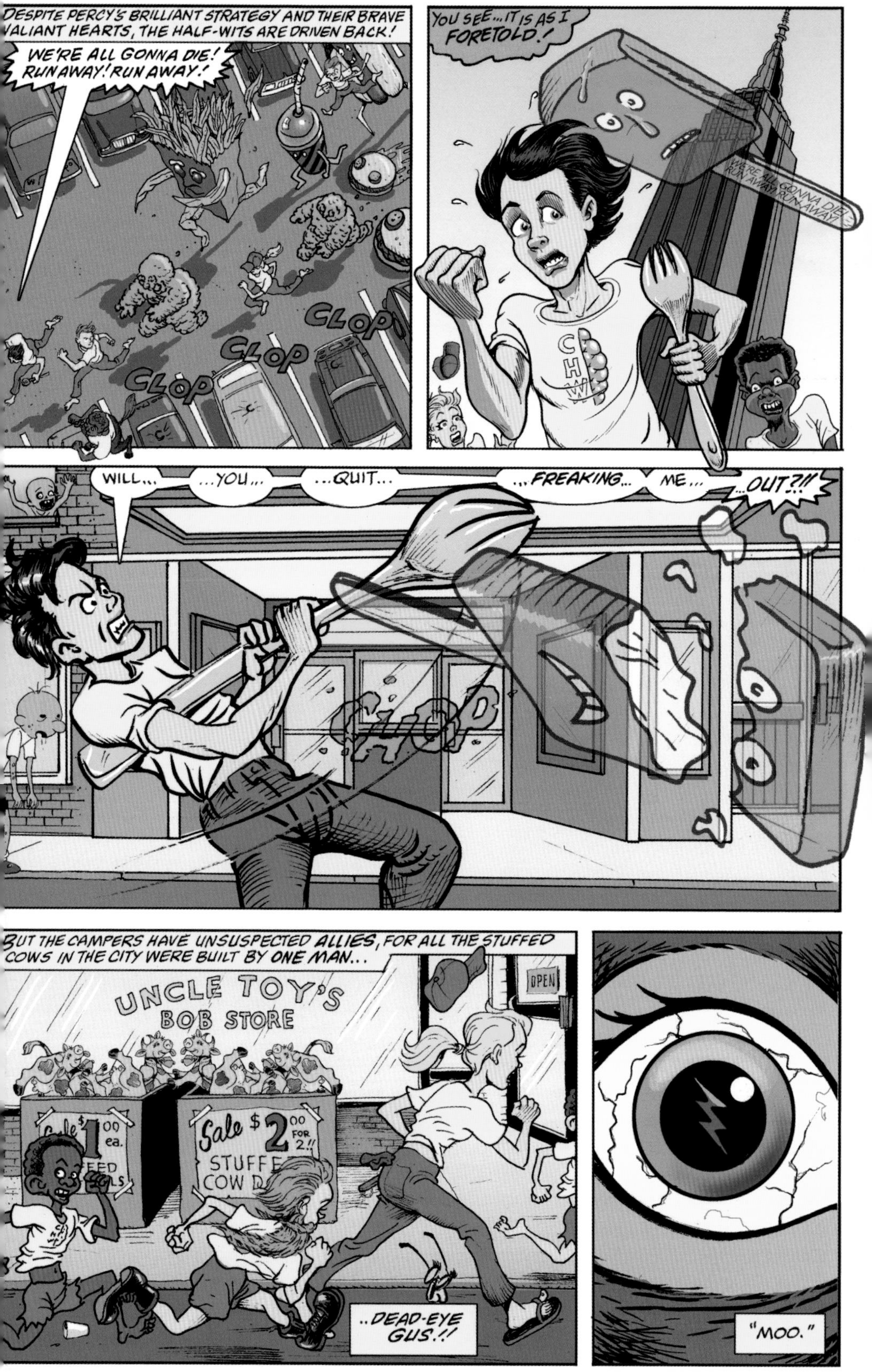
DESPITE PERCY'S BRILLIANT STRATEGY AND THEIR BRAVE VALIANT HEARTS, THE HALF-WITS ARE DRIVEN BACK!
WE'RE ALL GONNA DIE! RUN AWAY! RUN AWAY!
CLOP
CLOP
CLOP
YOU SEE...IT IS AS I FORETOLD!
WE'RE ALL GONNA DIE! RUN AWAY! RUN AWAY!
WILL...
...YOU...
...QUIT...
...FREAKING...
ME...
...OUT?!!
CHOP
BUT THE CAMPERS HAVE UNSUSPECTED ALLIES, FOR ALL THE STUFFED COWS IN THE CITY WERE BUILT BY ONE MAN...
UNCLE TOY'S BOB STORE
OPEN
Sale $2.00 FOR 2.!!
..DEAD-EYE GUS.!!
"MOO."

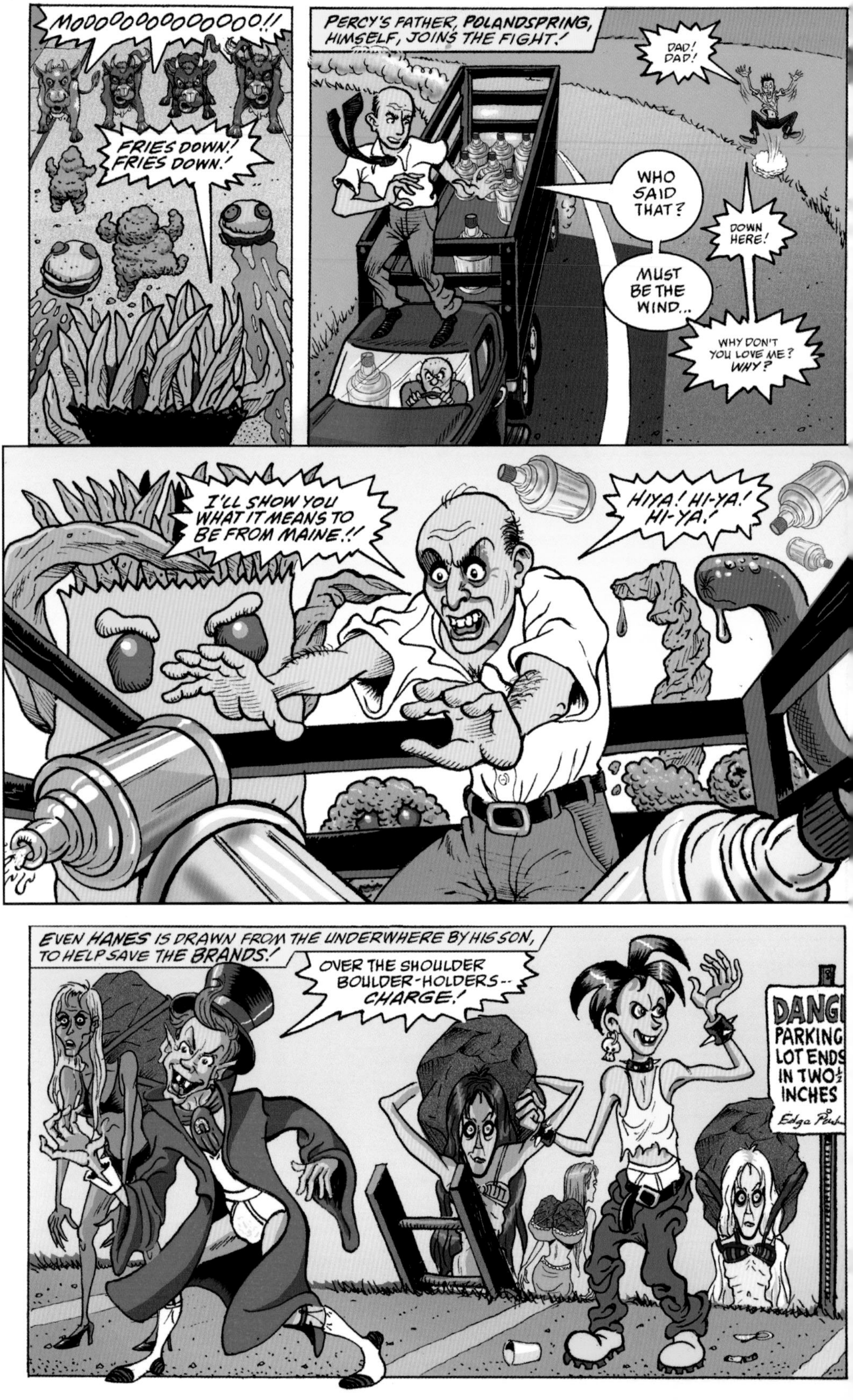
MOOOOOOOOOOOOOO!!
FRIES DOWN! FRIES DOWN!
PERCY'S FATHER, POLANDSPRING, HIMSELF, JOINS THE FIGHT!
DAD! DAD!
WHO SAID THAT?
MUST BE THE WIND...
DOWN HERE!
WHY DON'T YOU LOVE ME? WHY?
I'LL SHOW YOU WHAT IT MEANS TO BE FROM MAINE!!
HIYA! HI-YA! HI-YA!
EVEN HANES IS DRAWN FROM THE UNDERWHERE BY HIS SON, TO HELP SAVE THE BRANDS!
OVER THE SHOULDER BOULDER-HOLDERS-- CHARGE!
DANG
PARKING LOT ENDS IN TWO½ INCHES

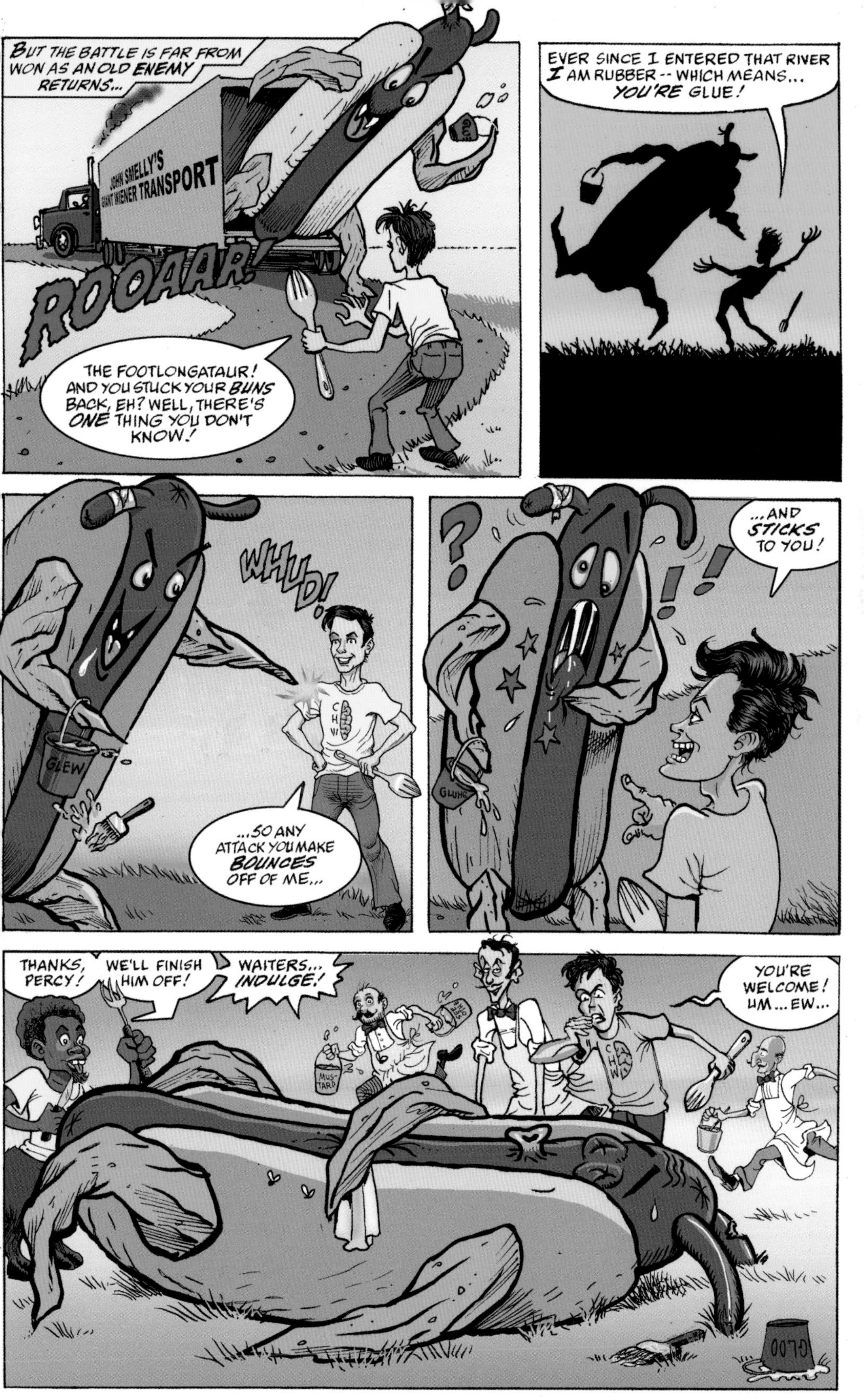

BUT THE BATTLE IS FAR FROM WON AS AN OLD ENEMY RETURNS...
JOHN SMELLY'S GIANT WIENER TRANSPORT
ROOAAR!
THE FOOTLONGATAUR! AND YOU STUCK YOUR BUNS BACK, EH? WELL, THERE'S ONE THING YOU DON'T KNOW!
EVER SINCE I ENTERED THAT RIVER I AM RUBBER -- WHICH MEANS... YOU'RE GLUE!
WHUD!
GLEW
...SO ANY ATTACK YOU MAKE BOUNCES OFF OF ME...
?
!!
...AND STICKS TO YOU!
GLUHG
THANKS, PERCY!
WE'LL FINISH HIM OFF!
WAITERS... INDULGE!
YOU'RE WELCOME! UM... EW...
MUSTARD
GLOO

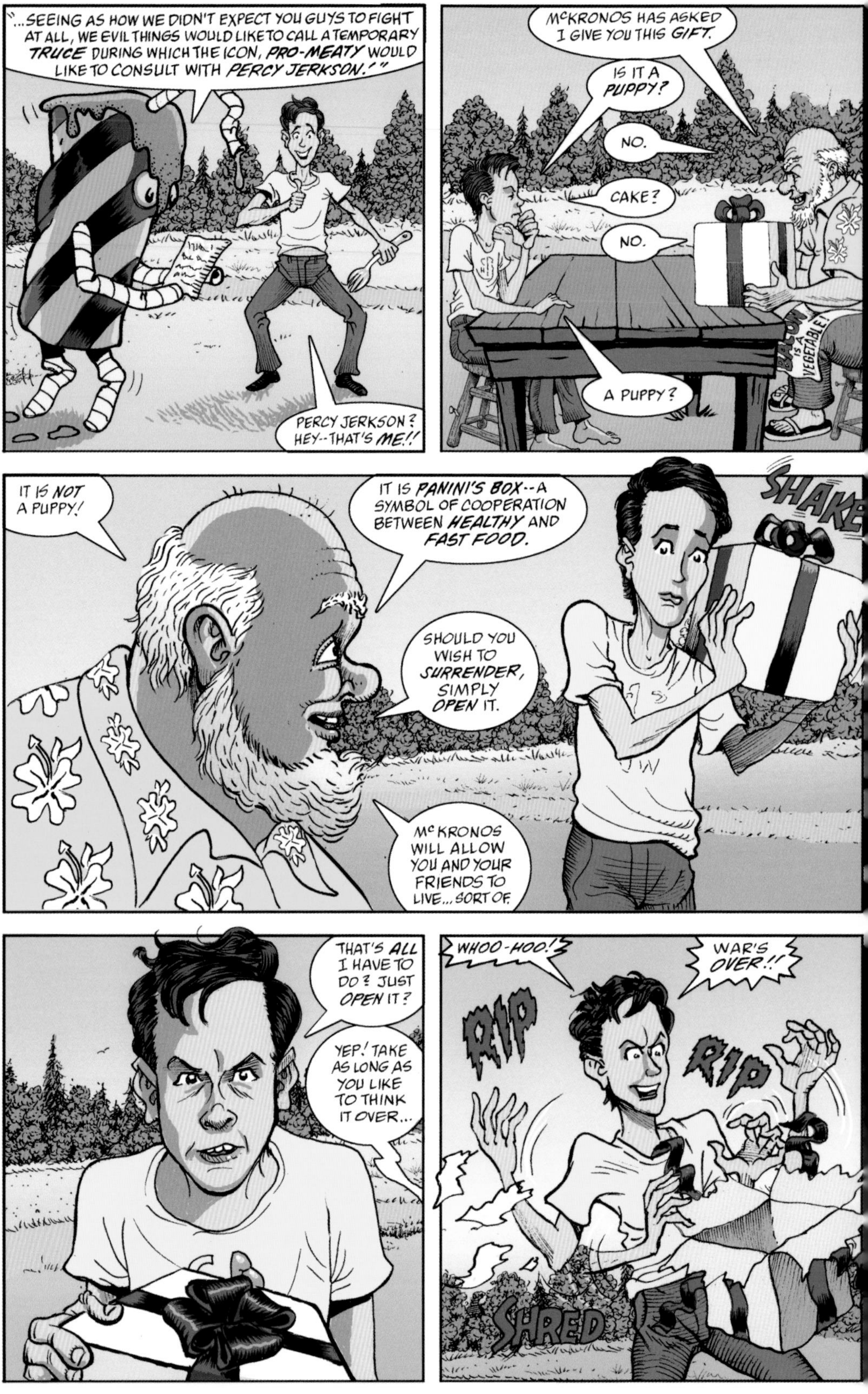
"...SEEING AS HOW WE DIDN'T EXPECT YOU GUYS TO FIGHT AT ALL, WE EVIL THINGS WOULD LIKE TO CALL A TEMPORARY TRUCE DURING WHICH THE ICON, PRO-MEATY WOULD LIKE TO CONSULT WITH PERCY JERKSON.'"
PERCY JERKSON? HEY--THAT'S ME!!
McKRONOS HAS ASKED I GIVE YOU THIS GIFT.
IS IT A PUPPY?
NO.
CAKE?
NO.
A PUPPY?
BACON IS A VEGETABLE!
IT IS NOT A PUPPY!
IT IS PANINI'S BOX--A SYMBOL OF COOPERATION BETWEEN HEALTHY AND FAST FOOD.
SHOULD YOU WISH TO SURRENDER, SIMPLY OPEN IT.
McKRONOS WILL ALLOW YOU AND YOUR FRIENDS TO LIVE... SORT OF.
SHAKE
THAT'S ALL I HAVE TO DO? JUST OPEN IT?
YEP! TAKE AS LONG AS YOU LIKE TO THINK IT OVER...
WHOO-HOO!
WAR'S OVER!!
RIP
RIP
SHRED

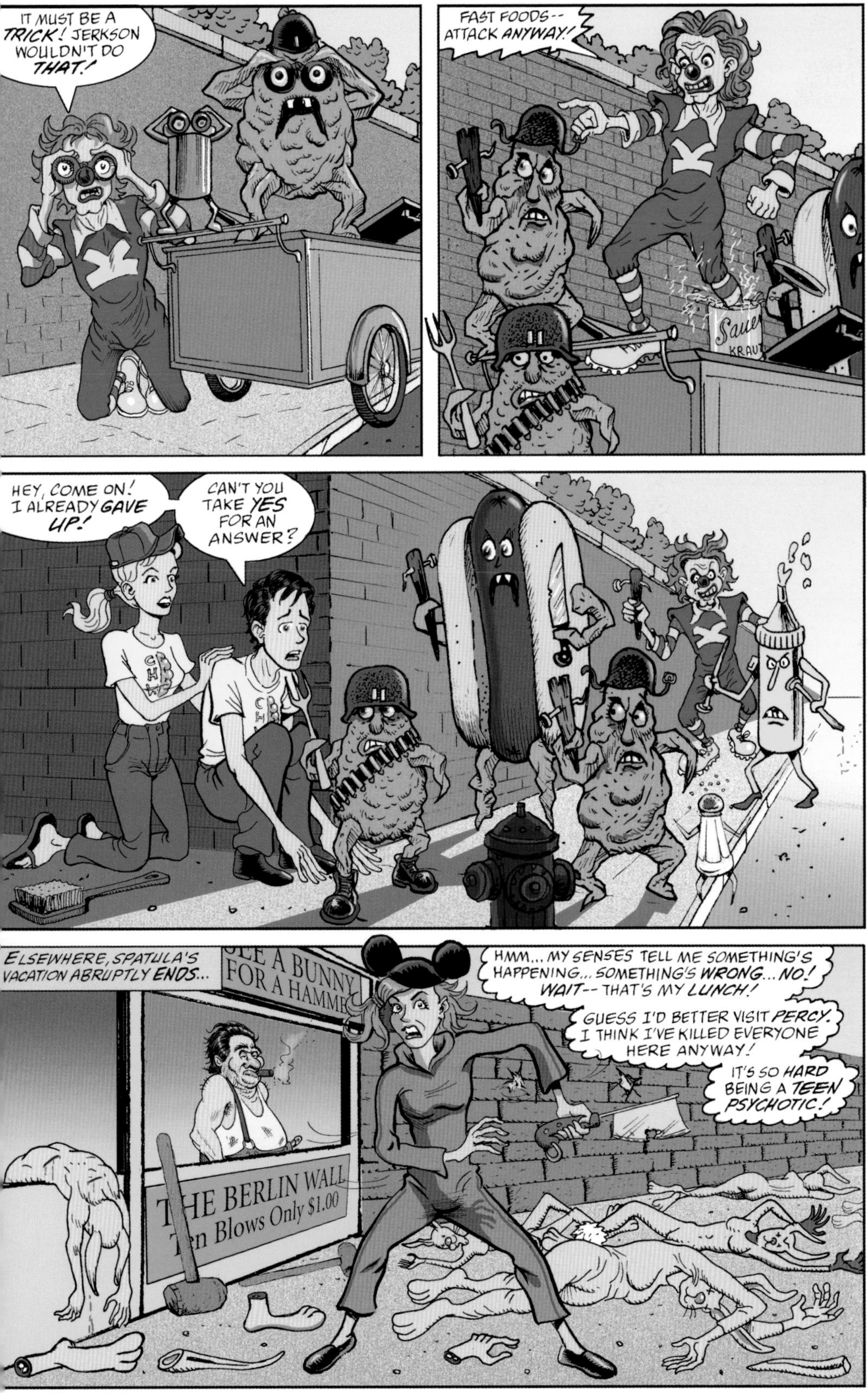
IT MUST BE A TRICK! JERKSON WOULDN'T DO THAT!
FAST FOODS-- ATTACK ANYWAY!
SAUER KRAUT
HEY, COME ON! I ALREADY GAVE UP!
CAN'T YOU TAKE YES FOR AN ANSWER?
ELSEWHERE, SPATULA'S VACATION ABRUPTLY ENDS...
SEE A BUNNY FOR A HAMM
HMM... MY SENSES TELL ME SOMETHING'S HAPPENING... SOMETHING'S WRONG... NO! WAIT-- THAT'S MY LUNCH!
GUESS I'D BETTER VISIT PERCY. I THINK I'VE KILLED EVERYONE HERE ANYWAY!
IT'S SO HARD BEING A TEEN PSYCHOTIC!
THE BERLIN WALL
Ten Blows Only $1.00

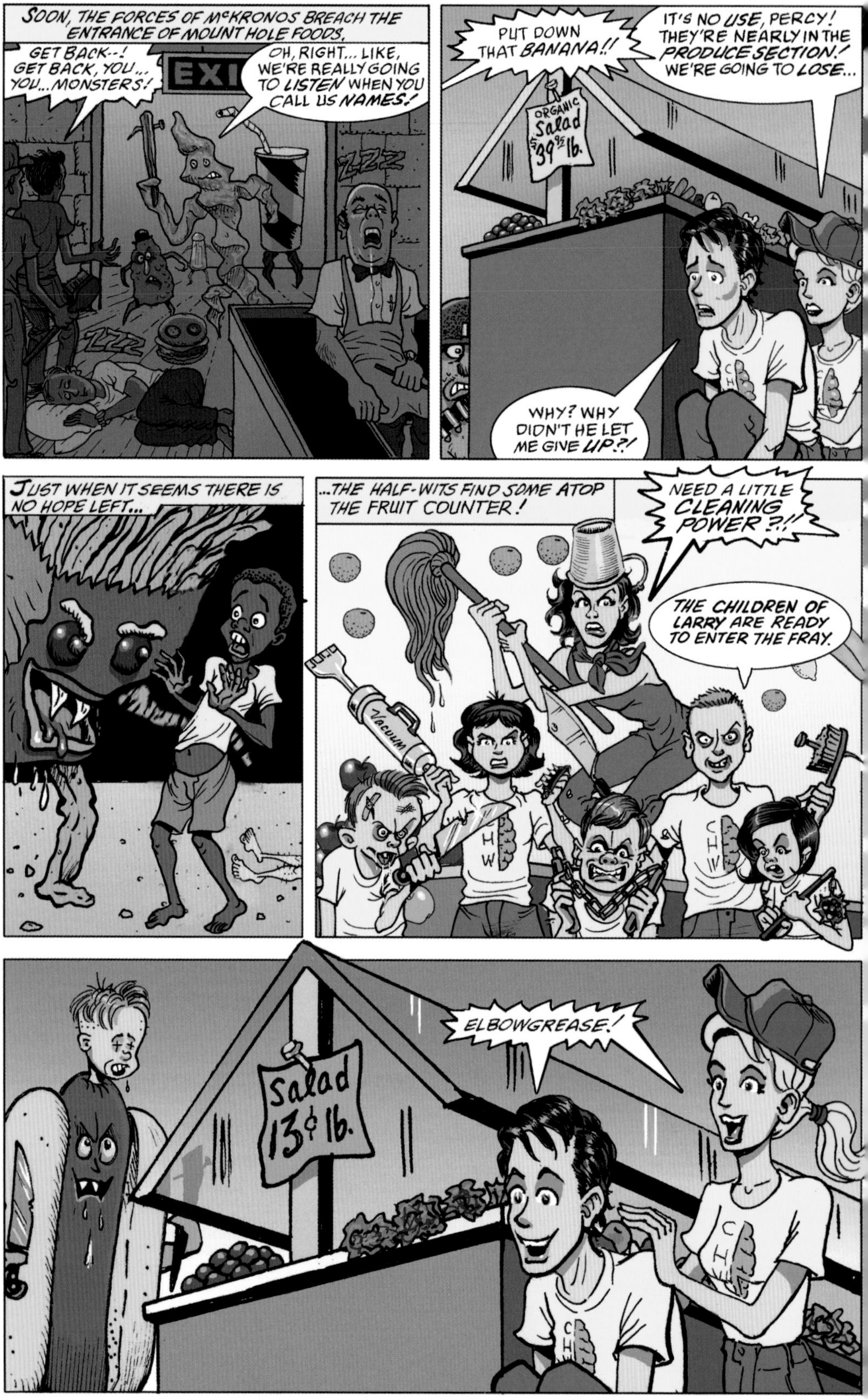
SOON, THE FORCES OF McKRONOS BREACH THE ENTRANCE OF MOUNT HOLE FOODS.
GET BACK--! GET BACK, YOU... YOU... MONSTERS!
EXI
OH, RIGHT... LIKE, WE'RE REALLY GOING TO LISTEN WHEN YOU CALL US NAMES!
ZZZ
ZZZ
PUT DOWN THAT BANANA!!
IT'S NO USE, PERCY! THEY'RE NEARLY IN THE PRODUCE SECTION! WE'RE GOING TO LOSE...
ORGANIC Salad $39.95 lb.
WHY? WHY DIDN'T HE LET ME GIVE UP?!
JUST WHEN IT SEEMS THERE IS NO HOPE LEFT...
...THE HALF-WITS FIND SOME ATOP THE FRUIT COUNTER!
NEED A LITTLE CLEANING POWER?!!
THE CHILDREN OF LARRY ARE READY TO ENTER THE FRAY.
Vacuum
ELBOWGREASE!
Salad 13¢ lb.

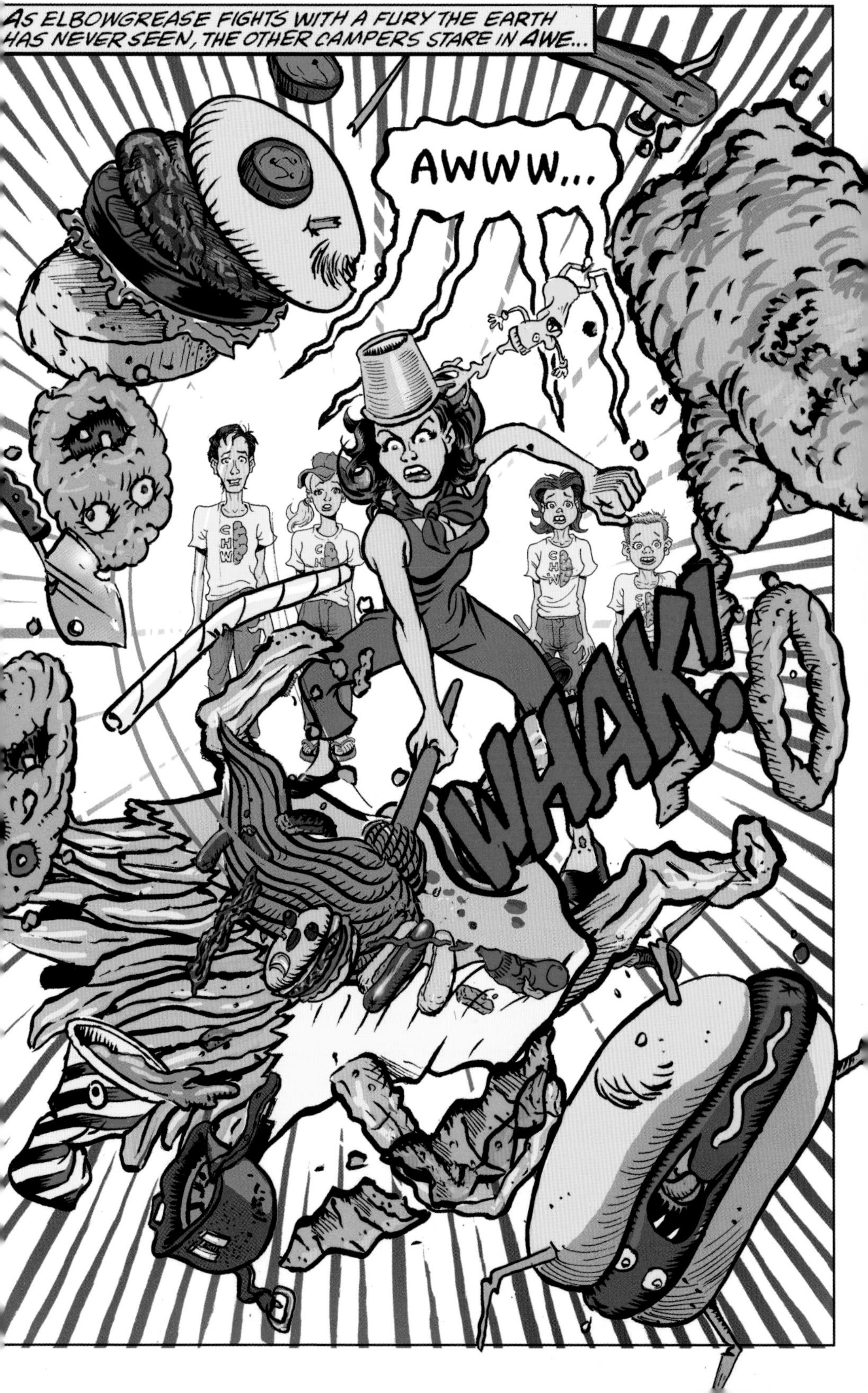
AS ELBOWGREASE FIGHTS WITH A FURY THE EARTH HAS NEVER SEEN, THE OTHER CAMPERS STARE IN AWE...
AWWW...
WHAK!

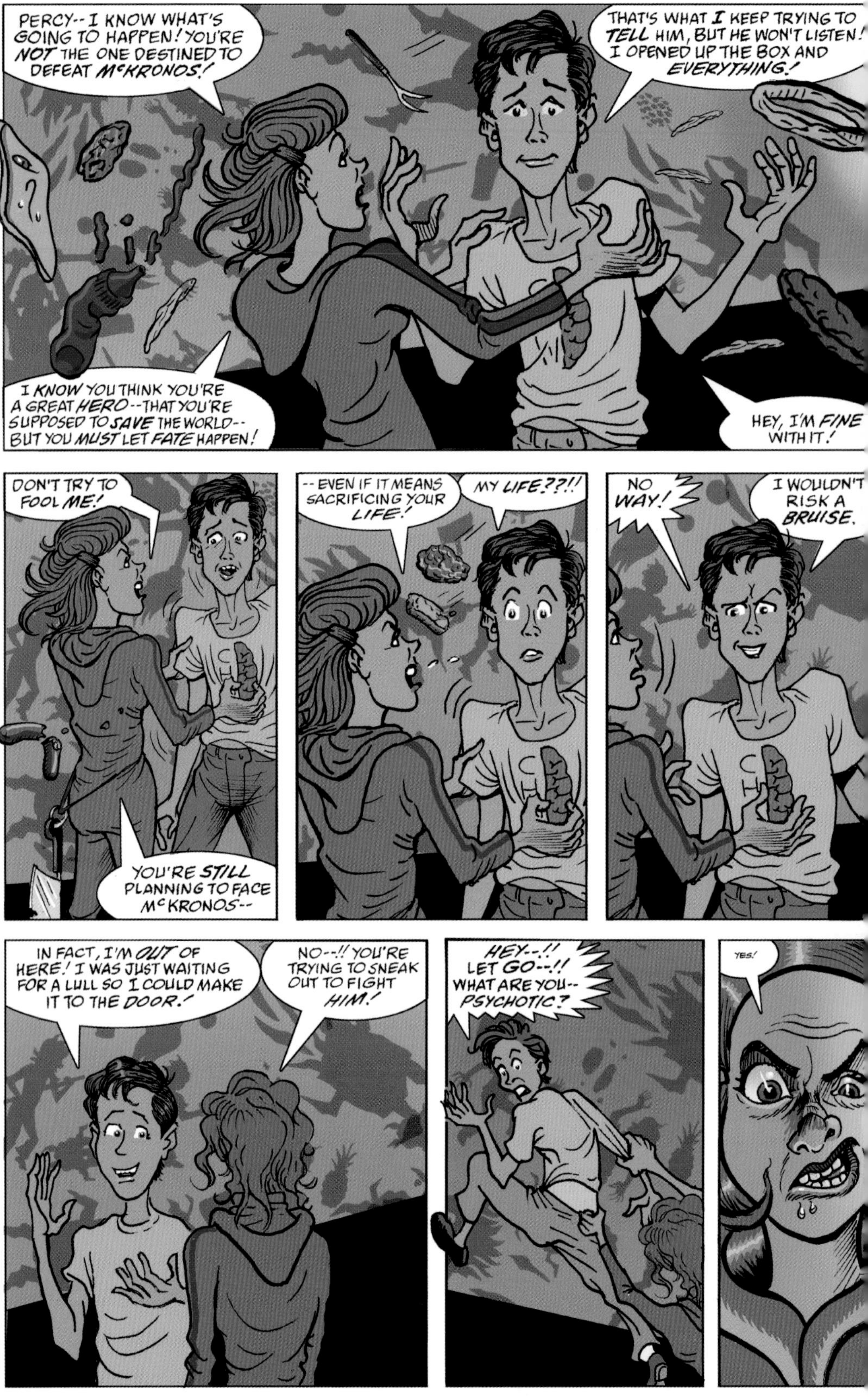
PERCY-- I KNOW WHAT'S GOING TO HAPPEN! YOU'RE NOT THE ONE DESTINED TO DEFEAT McKRONOS!
THAT'S WHAT I KEEP TRYING TO TELL HIM, BUT HE WON'T LISTEN! I OPENED UP THE BOX AND EVERYTHING!
I KNOW YOU THINK YOU'RE A GREAT HERO--THAT YOU'RE SUPPOSED TO SAVE THE WORLD-- BUT YOU MUST LET FATE HAPPEN!
HEY, I'M FINE WITH IT!
DON'T TRY TO FOOL ME!
YOU'RE STILL PLANNING TO FACE McKRONOS--
--EVEN IF IT MEANS SACRIFICING YOUR LIFE!
MY LIFE??!!
NO WAY!
I WOULDN'T RISK A BRUISE.
IN FACT, I'M OUT OF HERE! I WAS JUST WAITING FOR A LULL SO I COULD MAKE IT TO THE DOOR!
NO--!! YOU'RE TRYING TO SNEAK OUT TO FIGHT HIM!
HEY--!! LET GO--!! WHAT ARE YOU-- PSYCHOTIC?
YES!

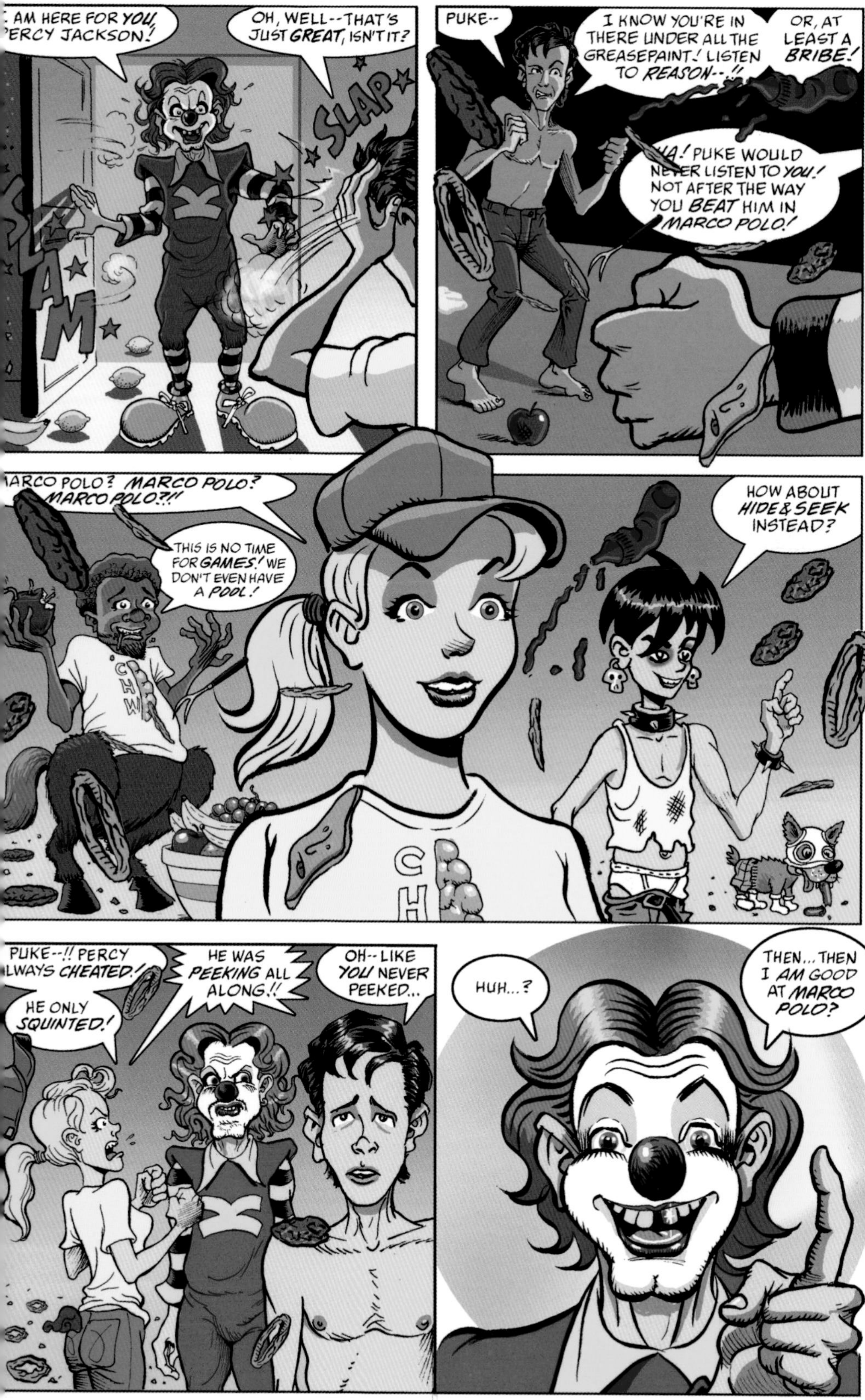
I AM HERE FOR YOU, PERCY JACKSON!
OH, WELL--THAT'S JUST GREAT, ISN'T IT?
SLAP
SLAM
PUKE--
I KNOW YOU'RE IN THERE UNDER ALL THE GREASEPAINT! LISTEN TO REASON--!!
OR, AT LEAST A BRIBE!
HA! PUKE WOULD NEVER LISTEN TO YOU! NOT AFTER THE WAY YOU BEAT HIM IN MARCO POLO!
MARCO POLO? MARCO POLO? MARCO POLO?!!
THIS IS NO TIME FOR GAMES! WE DON'T EVEN HAVE A POOL!
HOW ABOUT HIDE & SEEK INSTEAD?
PUKE--!! PERCY ALWAYS CHEATED!
HE ONLY SQUINTED!
HE WAS PEEKING ALL ALONG!!
OH--LIKE YOU NEVER PEEKED...
HUH...?
THEN... THEN I AM GOOD AT MARCO POLO?

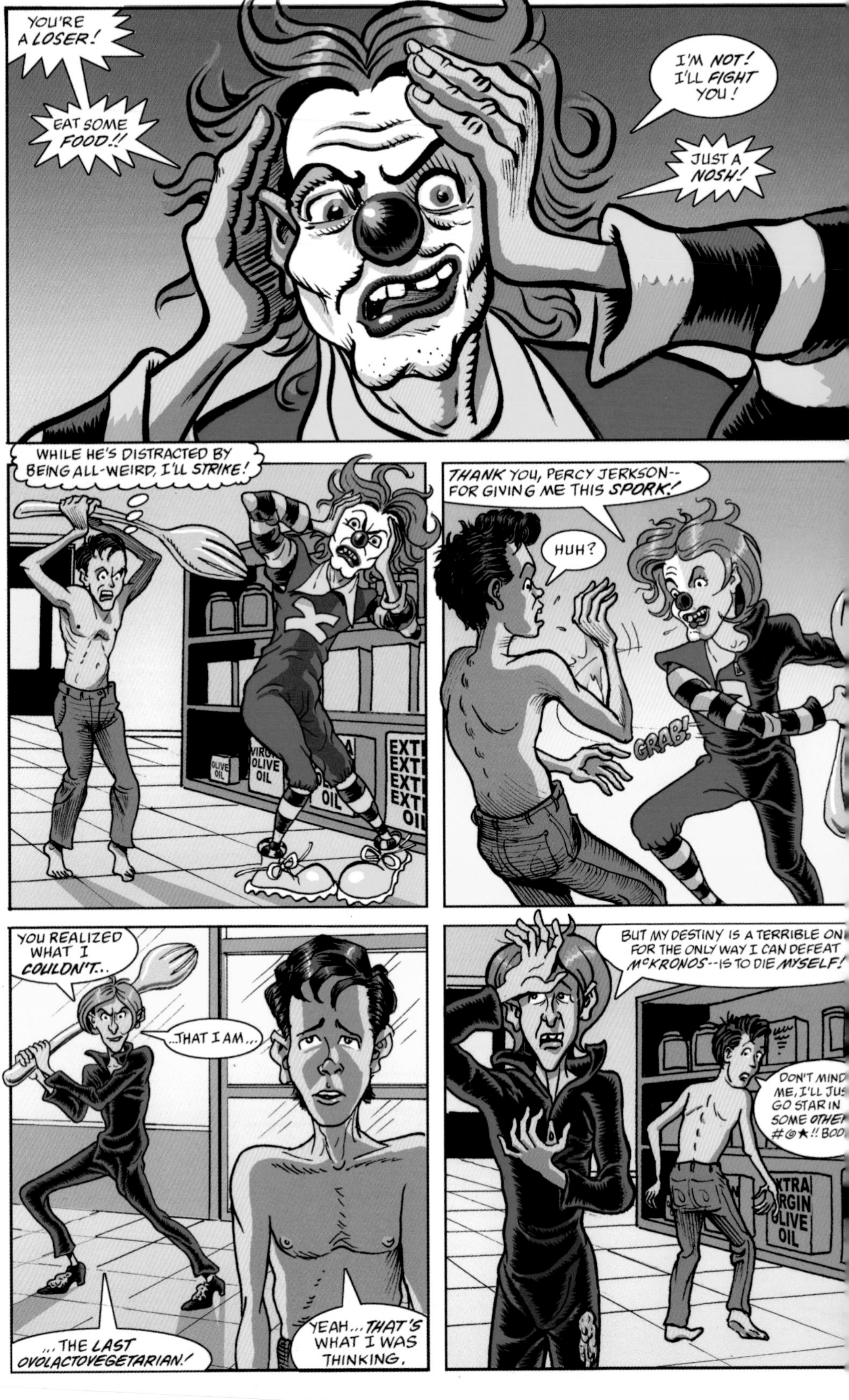
YOU'RE A LOSER!
EAT SOME FOOD!!
I'M NOT! I'LL FIGHT YOU!
JUST A NOSH!
WHILE HE'S DISTRACTED BY BEING ALL-WEIRD, I'LL STRIKE!
OLIVE OIL
THANK YOU, PERCY JERKSON-- FOR GIVING ME THIS SPORK!
HUH?
GRAB!
YOU REALIZED WHAT I COULDN'T...
...THAT I AM...
...THE LAST OVOLACTOVEGETARIAN!
YEAH... THAT'S WHAT I WAS THINKING.
BUT MY DESTINY IS A TERRIBLE ON
FOR THE ONLY WAY I CAN DEFEAT McKRONOS--IS TO DIE MYSELF!
DON'T MIND ME, I'LL JUS GO STAR IN SOME OTHE #@★!! BOD
EXTRA RGIN OLIVE OIL

THIS ENDS... *NOW!*

WOW! HE'S EATING AN ENTIRE MEAL OF ONLY *DAIRY* AND *VEGGIES!*

THE *LAST* OVOLACTOVEGETARIAN? I THINK HE MAY BE THE *ONLY* OVO-LACTOVEGETARIAN IN THIS BOOK!

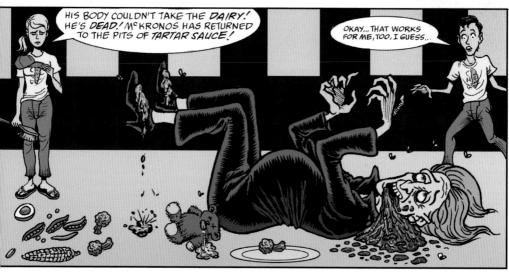

HIS BODY COULDN'T TAKE THE *DAIRY!* HE'S *DEAD!* M⊆KRONOS HAS RETURNED TO THE PITS OF *TARTAR SAUCE!*

OKAY... THAT WORKS FOR ME, TOO, I GUESS...

SOON, THE GODS CAPTURE THE MONSTROUS HYPHEN...

AND TRAP HIM *FOREVER!*

THUD

HOLLY WOO D

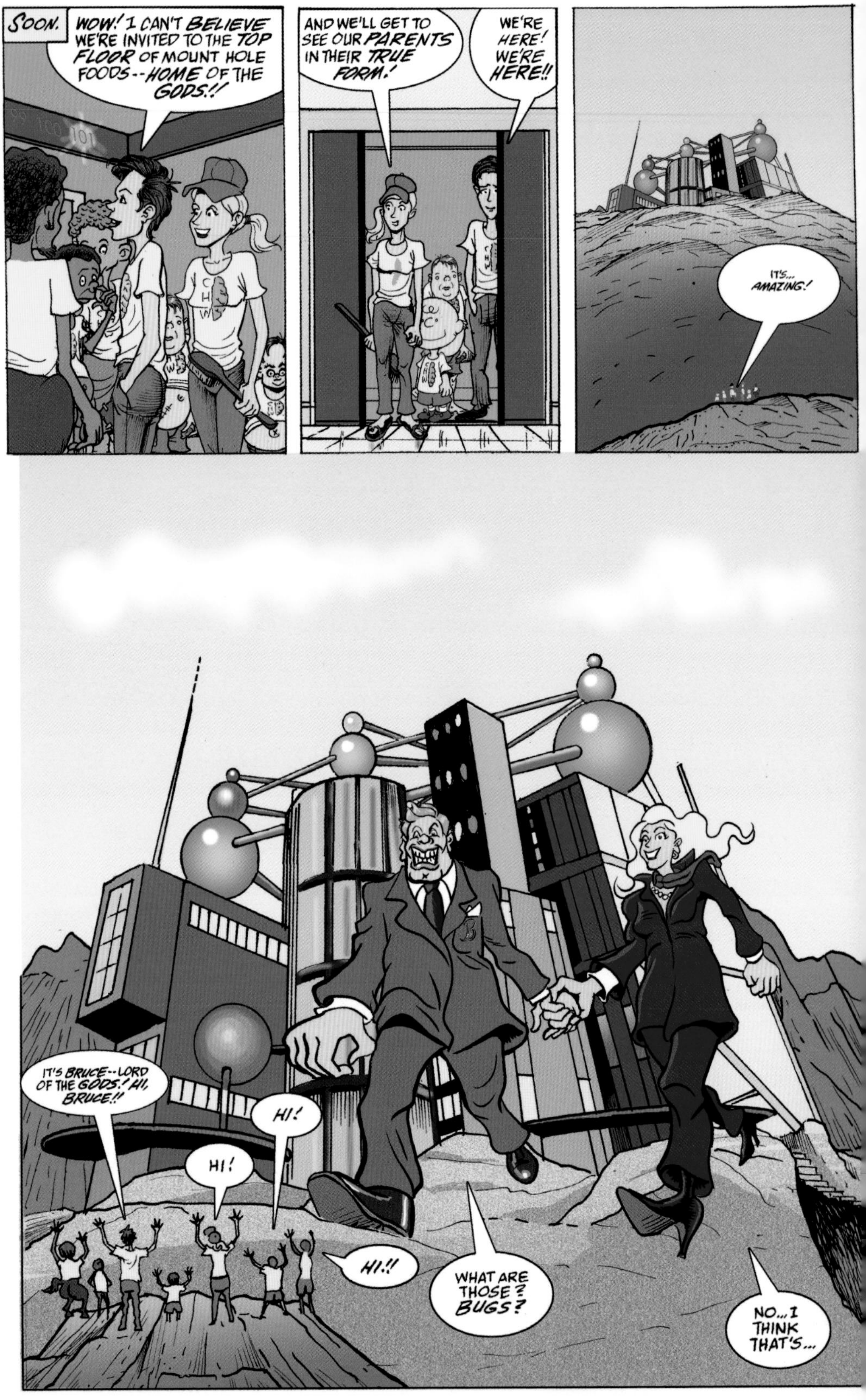
SOON.
WOW! I CAN'T BELIEVE WE'RE INVITED TO THE TOP FLOOR OF MOUNT HOLE FOODS--HOME OF THE GODS!!
AND WE'LL GET TO SEE OUR PARENTS IN THEIR TRUE FORM!
WE'RE HERE! WE'RE HERE!!
IT'S... AMAZING!
IT'S BRUCE--LORD OF THE GODS! HI, BRUCE!!
HI!
HI!
HI!!
WHAT ARE THOSE? BUGS?
NO... I THINK THAT'S...

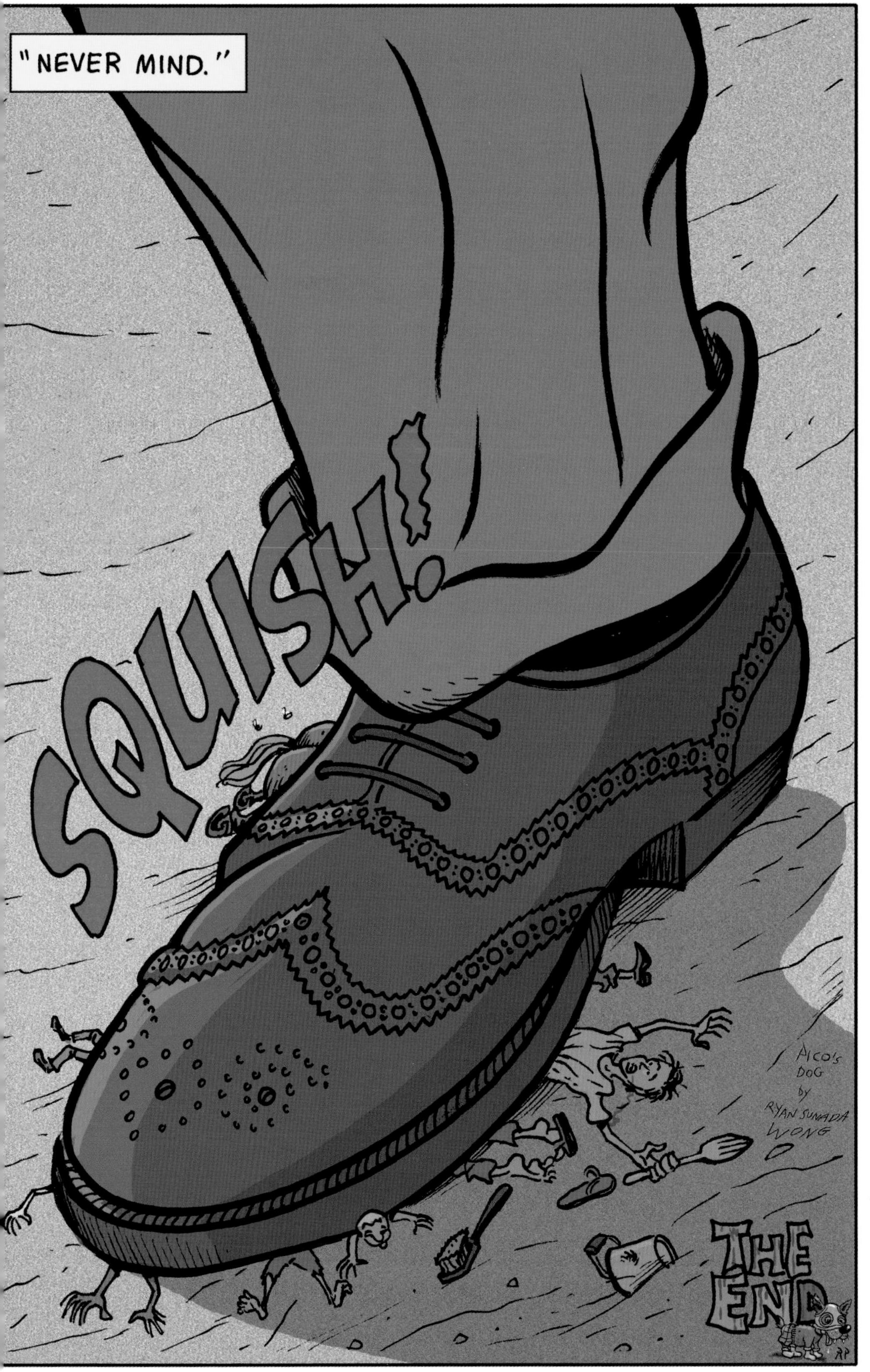
"NEVER MIND."
SQUISH!
PICO'S DOG by RYAN SUNADA WONG
THE END

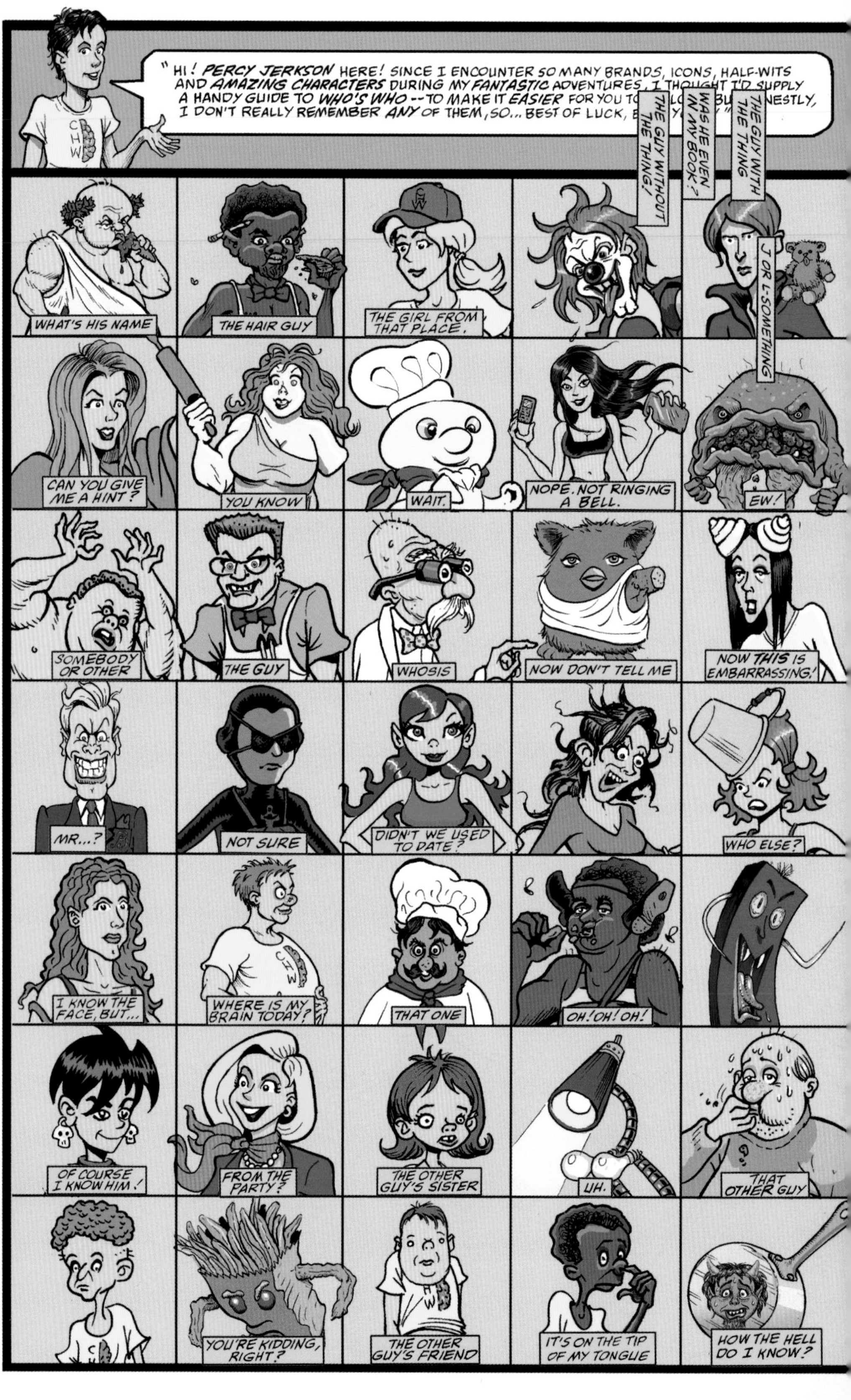
"HI! PERCY JERKSON HERE! SINCE I ENCOUNTER SO MANY BRANDS, ICONS, HALF-WITS
AND AMAZING CHARACTERS DURING MY FANTASTIC ADVENTURES, I THOUGHT I'D SUPPLY
A HANDY GUIDE TO WHO'S WHO --TO MAKE IT EASIER FOR YOU TO
NESTLY,
I DON'T REALLY REMEMBER ANY OF THEM, SO... BEST OF LUCK,
THE GUY WITHOUT THE THING!
WAS HE EVEN IN MY BOOK?
THE GUY WITH THE THING
WHAT'S HIS NAME
THE HAIR GUY
THE GIRL FROM THAT PLACE.
J OR L-SOMETHING
CAN YOU GIVE ME A HINT?
YOU KNOW
WAIT.
NOPE. NOT RINGING A BELL.
EW!
SOMEBODY OR OTHER
THE GUY
WHOSIS
NOW DON'T TELL ME
NOW THIS IS EMBARRASSING!
MR...?
NOT SURE
DIDN'T WE USED TO DATE?
WHO ELSE?
I KNOW THE FACE, BUT...
WHERE IS MY BRAIN TODAY?
THAT ONE
OH! OH! OH!
OF COURSE I KNOW HIM!
FROM THE PARTY?
THE OTHER GUY'S SISTER
UH.
THAT OTHER GUY
YOU'RE KIDDING, RIGHT?
THE OTHER GUY'S FRIEND
IT'S ON THE TIP OF MY TONGUE
HOW THE HELL DO I KNOW?

WATCH OUT FOR PAPERCUTZ

Welcome to the time-consuming and tactless third volume of PAPERCUTZ SLICES, the semi-new graphic novel series dedicated to poking fun at your favorite pop culture phenomenon and taking no prisoners. I'm Jim Salicrup, your foolish and mostly mortal Editor-in-Chief, here to attempt and explain, and if necessary, to even apologize, while plugging other Papercutz graphic novels.

If you're just joining us, then you're very lucky! Not because you didn't have to suffer through "Harry Potty and the Deathly Boring" or "breaking down," but because you can still purchase those prize examples of unauthorized parody at either your favorite bookseller (bookstore, online bookseller, or comics shop) or directly from Papercutz (see details on page 2).

If you've already picked up the previous PAPERCUTZ SLICES, and you're still looking for graphic novels that can tickle your funny bone, and you're already up to speed on THE SMURFS graphic novels by the legendary Peyo and the GARFIELD & Co graphic novels based on Jim Davis's lasagna-loving, fat cat, then maybe it's time we tell you about the latest and greatest graphic novels heading your way from Papercutz.

First, there's the touching tale of Nina… and Sybil, the fairy who lives in her backpack. Created by Michael Rodrigue, and beautifully illustrated by Antonello Dalena and Manuela Razzi, SYBIL THE BACKPACK FAIRY explores what would happen to a middle school girl, with a younger brother, a single mom, and who is bullied at school, if she had her very own fairy. Check out the preview on the next page, to get a small taste of how much fun the series will be.

Then, even though we love all our wonderful creators equally, we're especially proud to add the world-famous Lewis Trondheim to the terrific Papercutz talent pool. His series is called MONSTER, and the first volume is called MONSTER CHRISTMAS. The series features an almost normal family and their almost ordinary adventures… and their pet monster. Check out the extra-long preview that starts in just a couple of pages!

Finally, we're offering a sneak peek as well at ERNEST & REBECCA. Rebecca is a 6 ½ year-old girl, and Ernest is her pet germ. Written by Guillamo Bianco, and illustrated by the very productive Antonello Dalena, it's another new series we suspect you'll laugh with and love! Check out the preview on our very last page.

And wait till you see what we have planned for PAPERCUTZ SLICES #4! Rather than just tell you what best-selling series we'll be spoofing next time, we'll just make a little GAME out of it. But if you really HUNGER for the answer, you'll just have to keep an eye on our website – www.papercutz.com– where you'll always find out the latest news!

So, until we meet again-- May the Farce be with you,

Jim

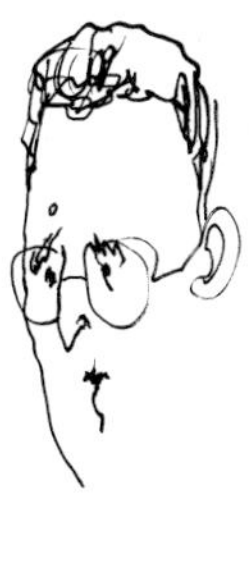

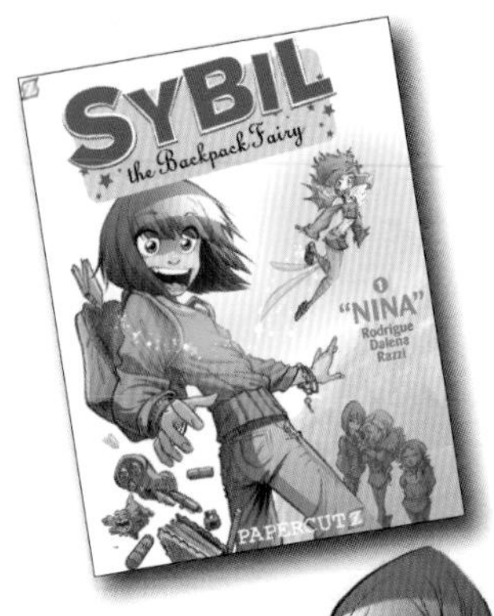
SYBIL
the Backpack Fairy
1
"NINA"
Rodrigue
Dalena
Razzi
PAPERCUTZ

Special preview of
SYBIL THE BACKPACK FAIRY #1 "Nina"

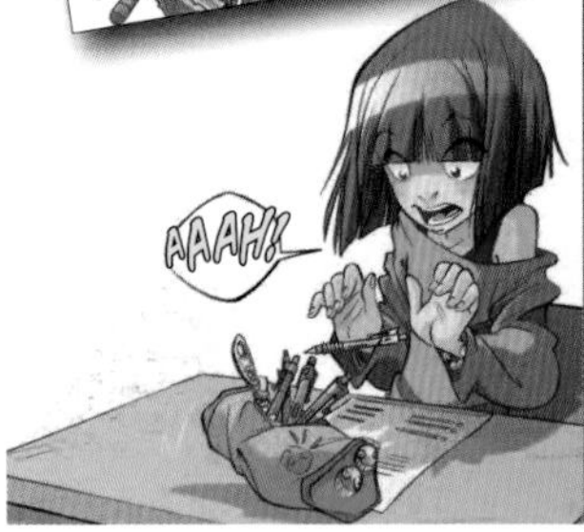
AAAH!

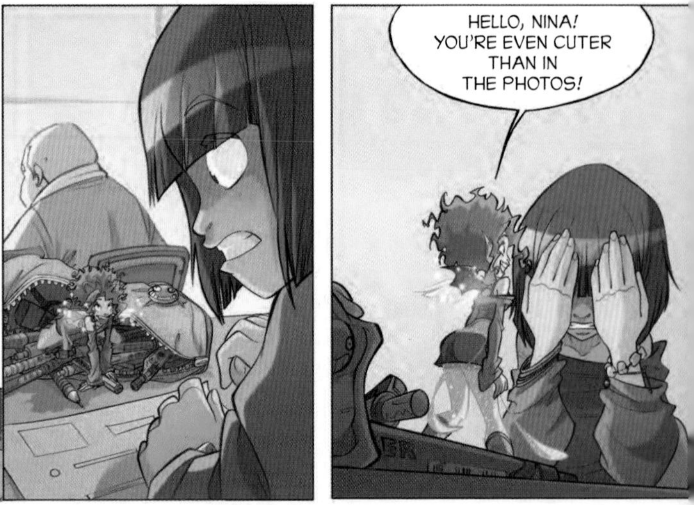
HELLO, NINA! YOU'RE EVEN CUTER THAN IN THE PHOTOS!

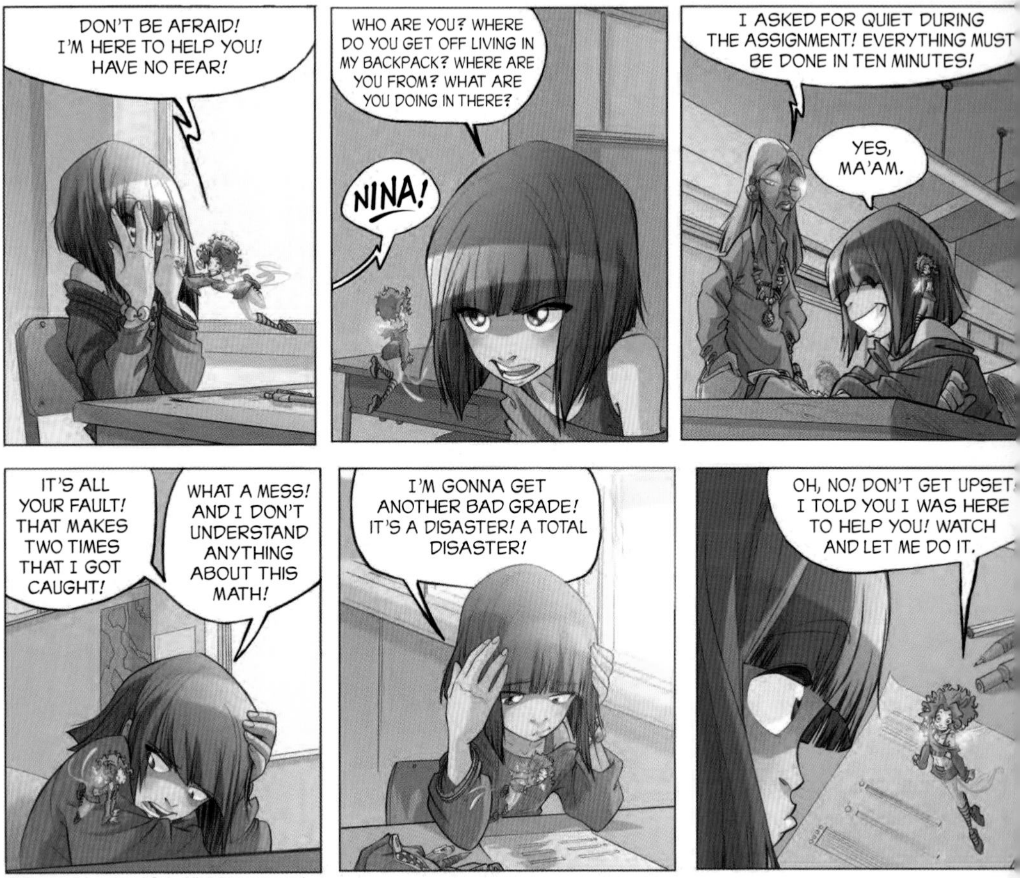
DON'T BE AFRAID! I'M HERE TO HELP YOU! HAVE NO FEAR!
WHO ARE YOU? WHERE DO YOU GET OFF LIVING IN MY BACKPACK? WHERE ARE YOU FROM? WHAT ARE YOU DOING IN THERE?
NINA!
I ASKED FOR QUIET DURING THE ASSIGNMENT! EVERYTHING MUST BE DONE IN TEN MINUTES!
YES, MA'AM.
IT'S ALL YOUR FAULT! THAT MAKES TWO TIMES THAT I GOT CAUGHT!
WHAT A MESS! AND I DON'T UNDERSTAND ANYTHING ABOUT THIS MATH!
I'M GONNA GET ANOTHER BAD GRADE! IT'S A DISASTER! A TOTAL DISASTER!
OH, NO! DON'T GET UPSET. I TOLD YOU I WAS HERE TO HELP YOU! WATCH AND LET ME DO IT.

SPECIAL PREVIEW OF
MONSTER CHRISTMAS by Lewis Trondheim…

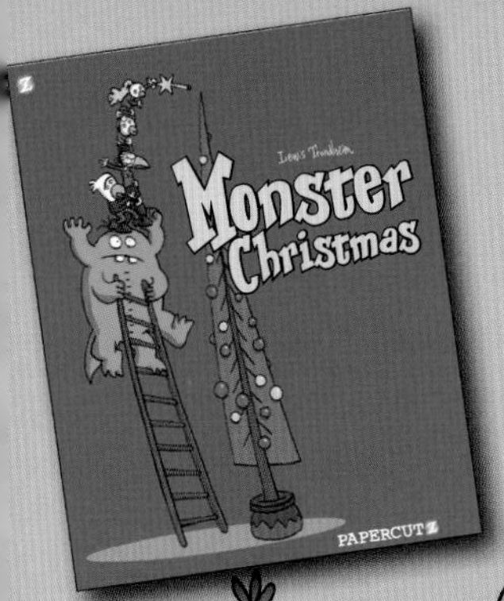
Lewis Trondheim
Monster Christmas
PAPERCUTZ

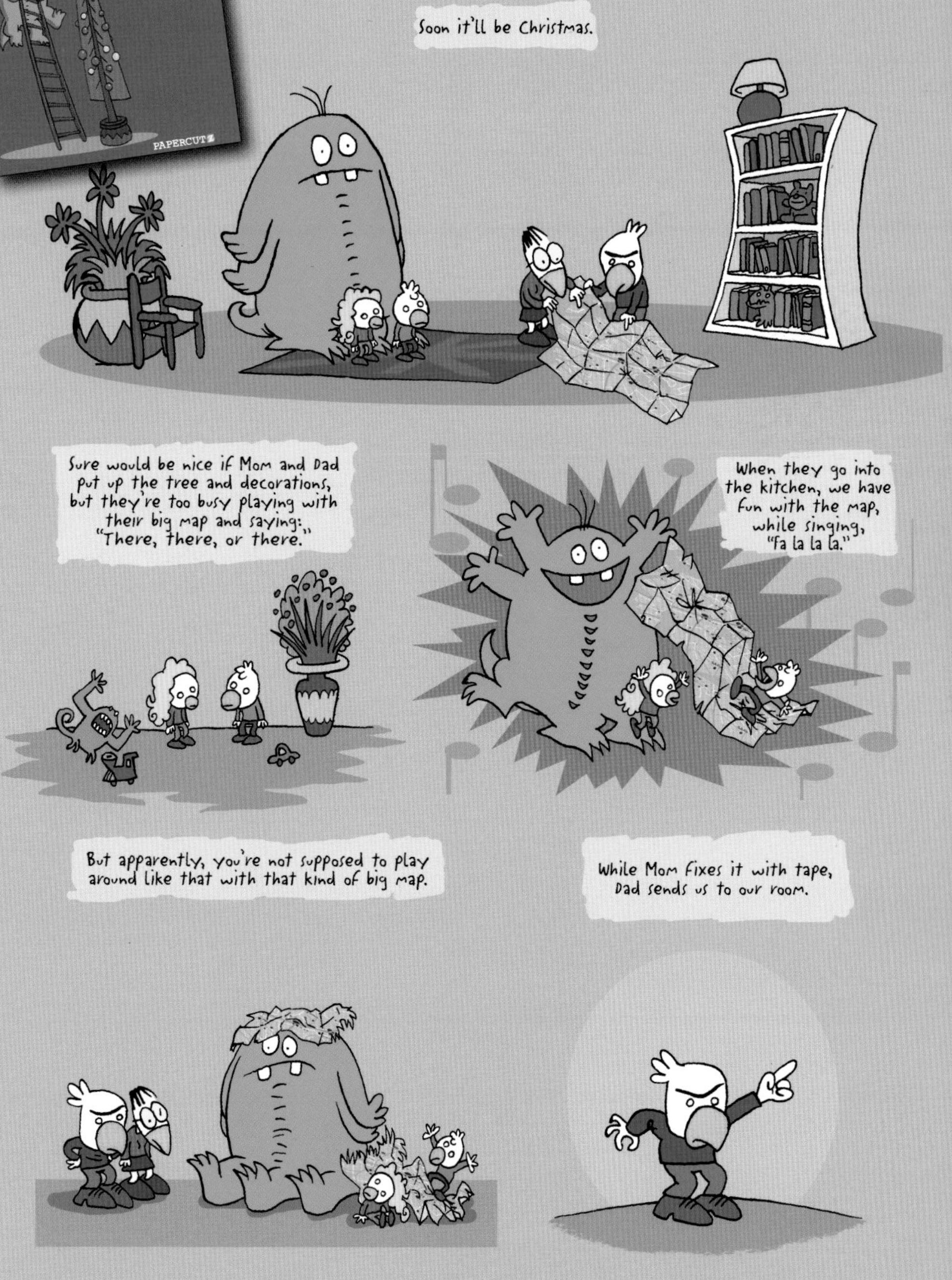
Soon it'll be Christmas.
Sure would be nice if Mom and Dad put up the tree and decorations, but they're too busy playing with their big map and saying: "There, there, or there."
When they go into the kitchen, we have fun with the map, while singing, "Fa la la la."
But apparently, you're not supposed to play around like that with that kind of big map.
While Mom fixes it with tape, Dad sends us to our room.

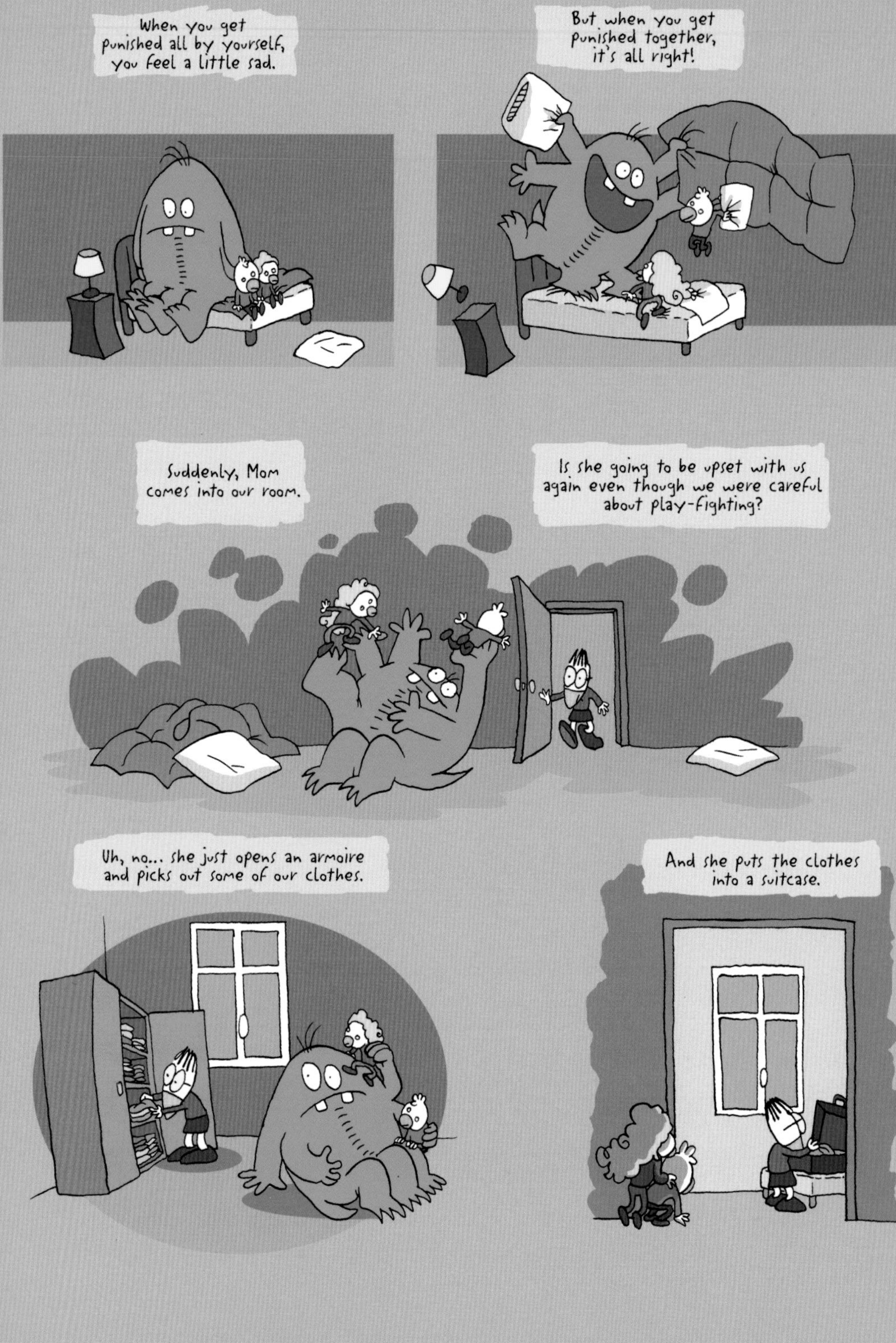
When you get punished all by yourself, you feel a little sad.
But when you get punished together, it's all right!
Suddenly, Mom comes into our room.
Is she going to be upset with us again even though we were careful about play-fighting?
Uh, no... she just opens an armoire and picks out some of our clothes.
And she puts the clothes into a suitcase.

Woo-hoo!
That means we're
going on vacation!

Or that Mom and Dad
are going to send us
to a boarding school
far from home.

Or that our clothes are
too little because we've grown
a lot, and now we can go to
the movies all on
our own.

Or that she's making
room in the armoire
to shut us inside when
we're not good!

Or that each of
us will have a room
all to ourselves...

Or that there's going to be
a huge earthquake and we've
got to move away real quick!

  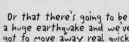

Or that some huge, giant
monsters are going to fight
in the street and the
neighborhood has to be
evacuated.

Mom tells us, in fact, that we're going to go on vacation.
That's what we thought at first, but a monster
battle in the street would've been way cooler.

And that also means
we won't have a
pretty Christmas
tree in the house.

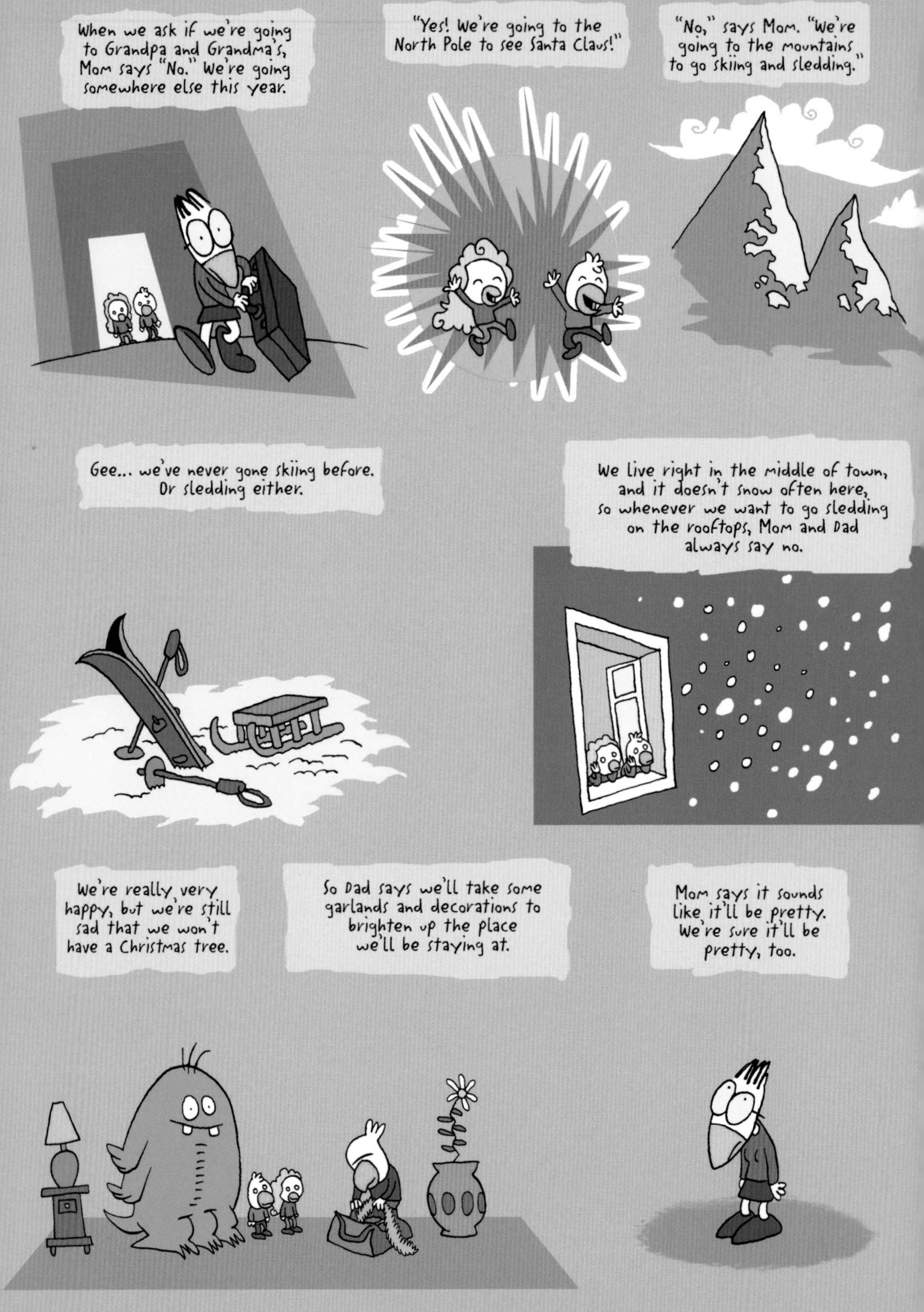
When we ask if we're going to Grandpa and Grandma's, Mom says "No." We're going somewhere else this year.
"Yes! We're going to the North Pole to see Santa Claus!"
"No," says Mom. "We're going to the mountains to go skiing and sledding."
Gee... we've never gone skiing before. Or sledding either.
We live right in the middle of town, and it doesn't snow often here, so whenever we want to go sledding on the rooftops, Mom and Dad always say no.
We're really very happy, but we're still sad that we won't have a Christmas tree.
So Dad says we'll take some garlands and decorations to brighten up the place we'll be staying at.
Mom says it sounds like it'll be pretty. We're sure it'll be pretty, too.

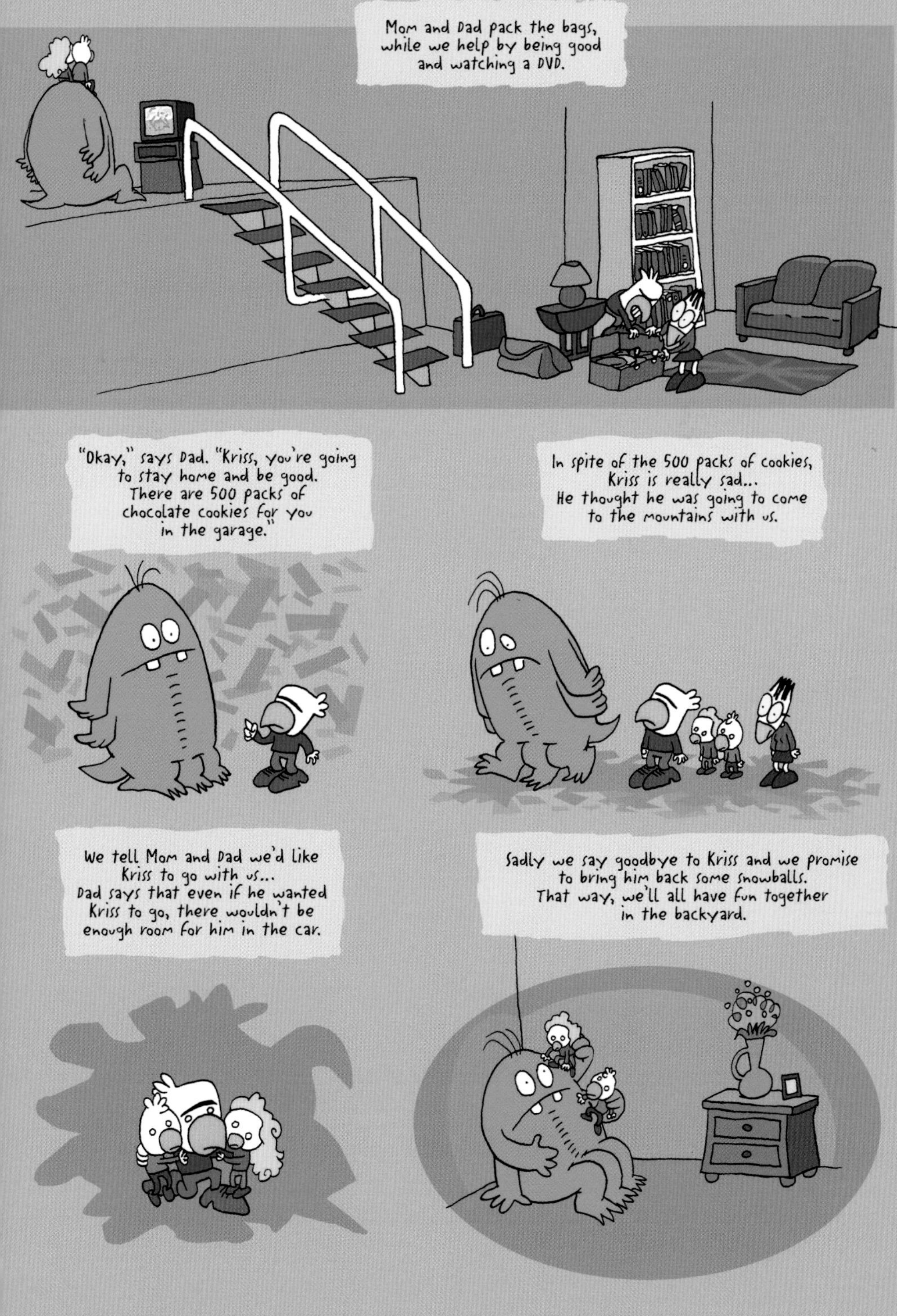
Mom and Dad pack the bags, while we help by being good and watching a DVD.
"Okay," says Dad. "Kriss, you're going to stay home and be good. There are 500 packs of chocolate cookies for you in the garage."
In spite of the 500 packs of cookies, Kriss is really sad... He thought he was going to come to the mountains with us.
We tell Mom and Dad we'd like Kriss to go with us... Dad says that even if he wanted Kriss to go, there wouldn't be enough room for him in the car.
Sadly we say goodbye to Kriss and we promise to bring him back some snowballs. That way, we'll all have fun together in the backyard.

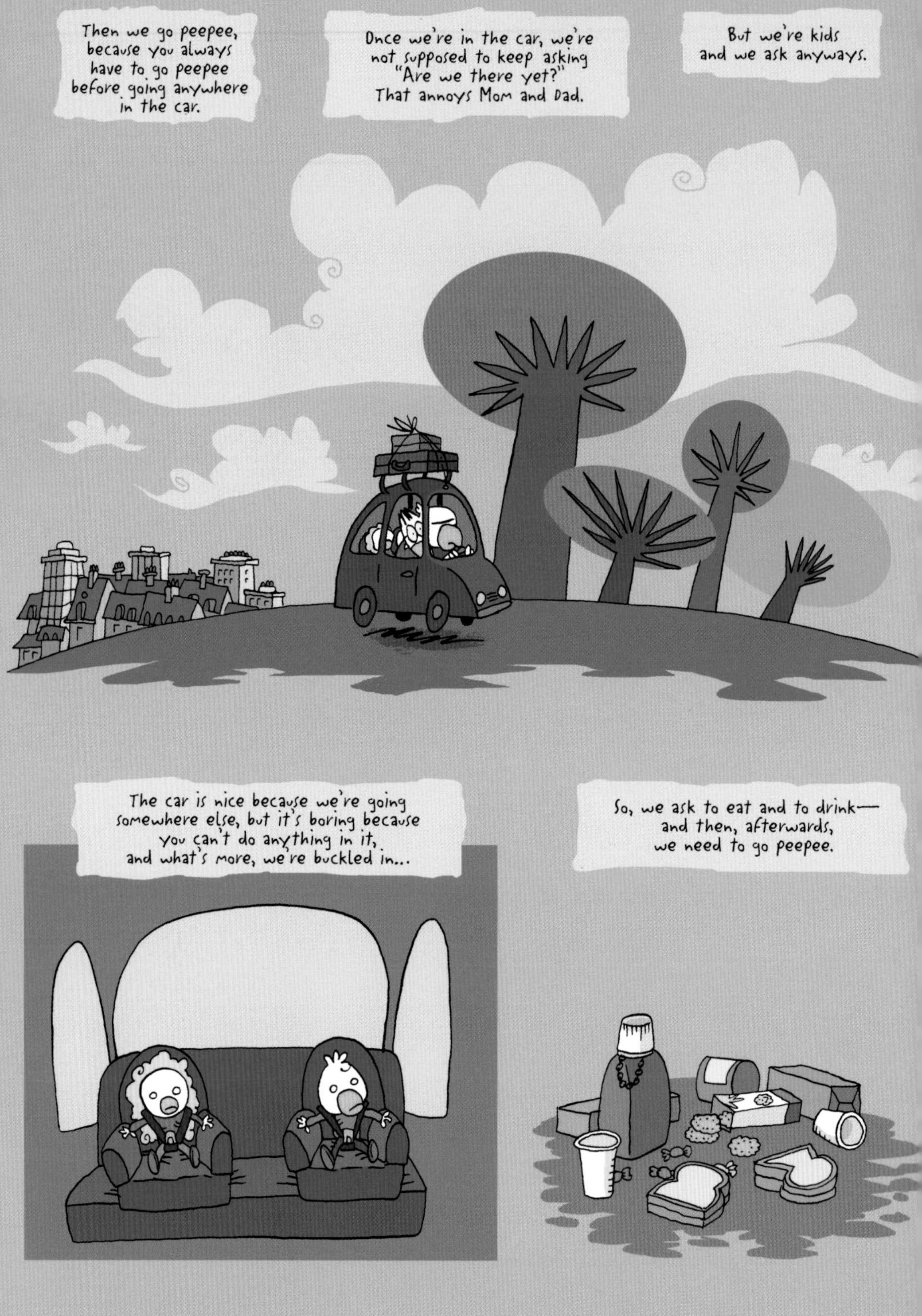
Then we go peepee, because you always have to go peepee before going anywhere in the car.
Once we're in the car, we're not supposed to keep asking "Are we there yet?" That annoys Mom and Dad.
But we're kids and we ask anyways.
The car is nice because we're going somewhere else, but it's boring because you can't do anything in it, and what's more, we're buckled in...
So, we ask to eat and to drink—and then, afterwards, we need to go peepee.

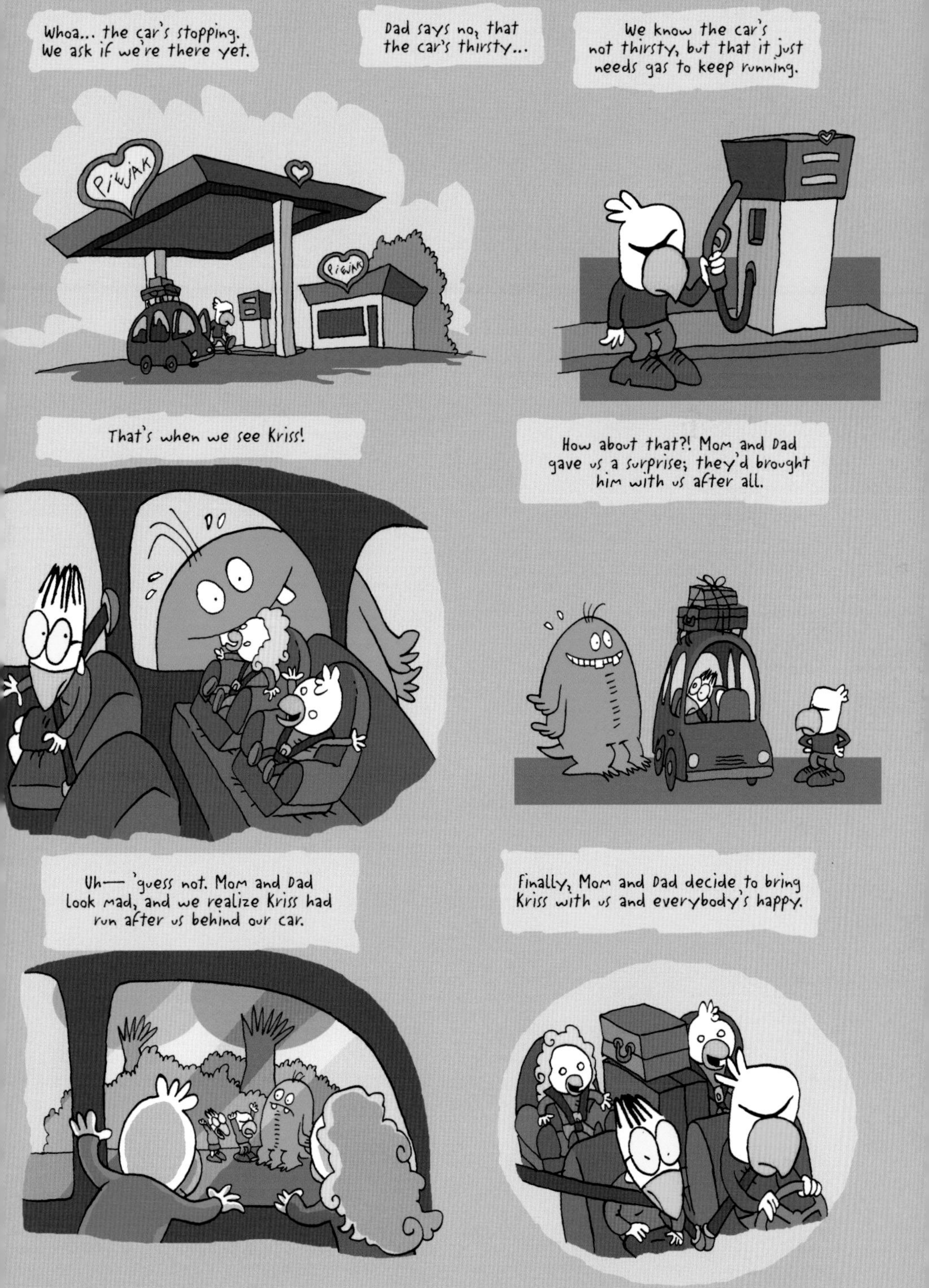

Whoa... the car's stopping. We ask if we're there yet.
Dad says no, that the car's thirsty...
We know the car's not thirsty, but that it just needs gas to keep running.
That's when we see Kriss!
How about that?! Mom and Dad gave us a surprise; they'd brought him with us after all.
Uh— 'guess not. Mom and Dad look mad, and we realize Kriss had run after us behind our car.
Finally, Mom and Dad decide to bring Kriss with us and everybody's happy.

Don't miss MONSTER CHRISTMAS coming September 2011!

Special preview of ERNEST & REBECCA #1 “My Best Friend is a Germ”

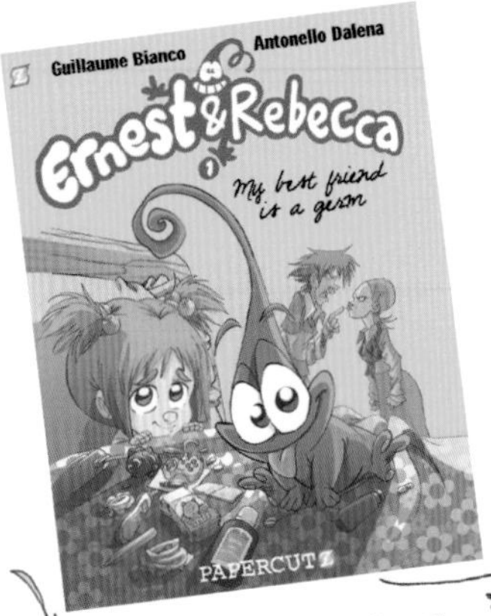

Guillaume Bianco
Antonello Dalena
Ernest & Rebecca
1
My best friend is a germ
PAPERCUTZ

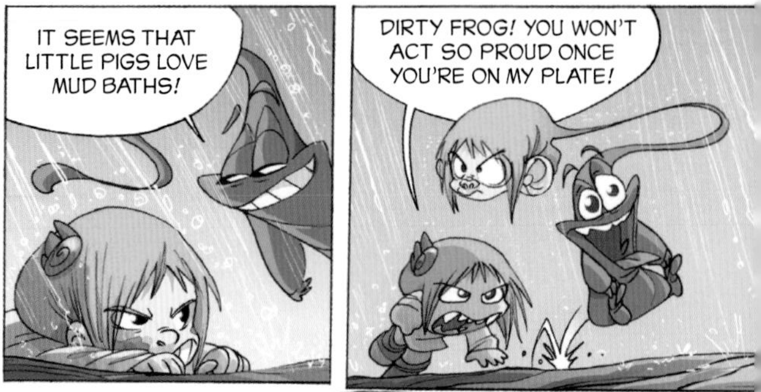

IT SEEMS THAT LITTLE PIGS LOVE MUD BATHS!
DIRTY FROG! YOU WON'T ACT SO PROUD ONCE YOU'RE ON MY PLATE!

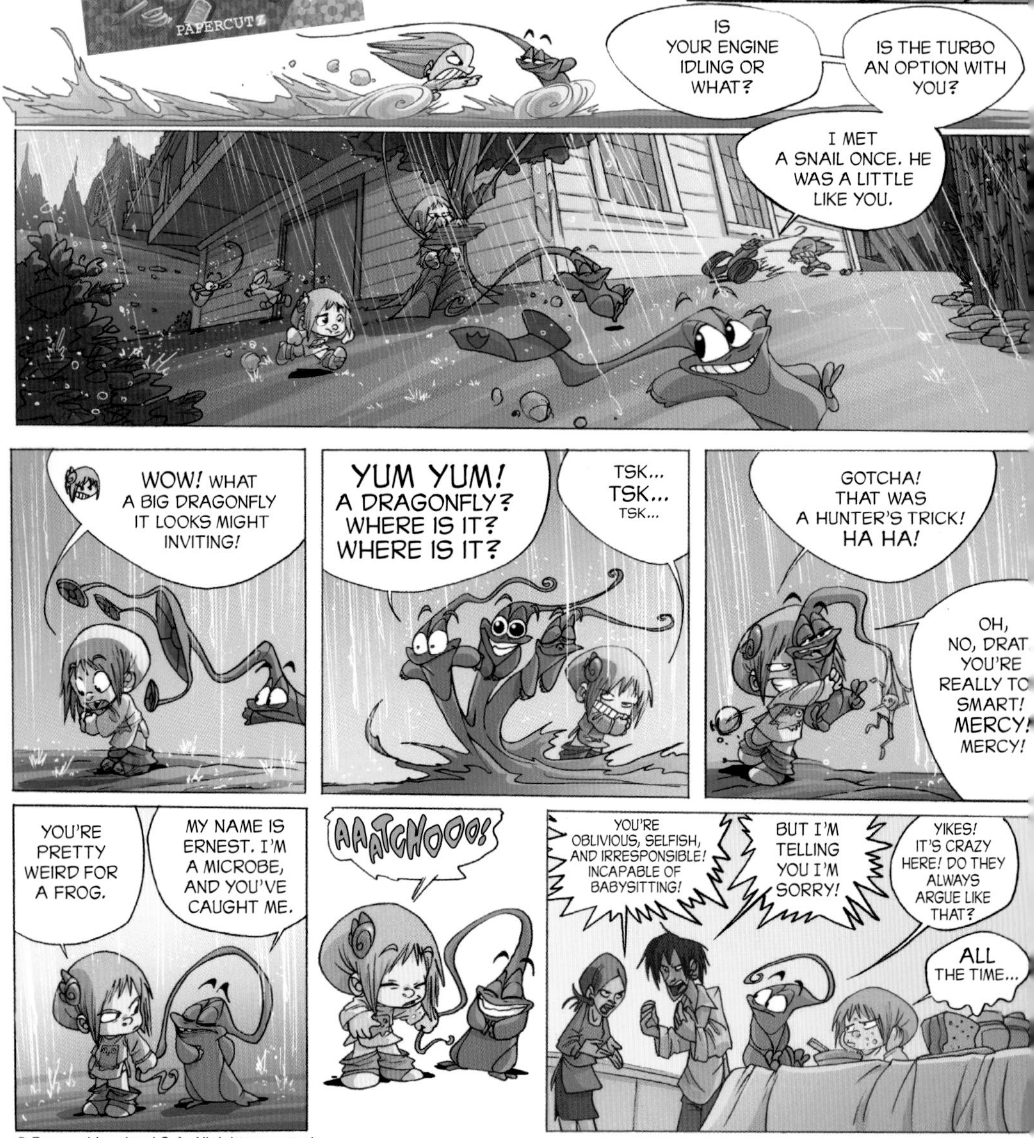

IS YOUR ENGINE IDLING OR WHAT?
IS THE TURBO AN OPTION WITH YOU?
I MET A SNAIL ONCE. HE WAS A LITTLE LIKE YOU.
WOW! WHAT A BIG DRAGONFLY IT LOOKS MIGHT INVITING!
YUM YUM! A DRAGONFLY? WHERE IS IT? WHERE IS IT?
TSK... TSK... TSK...
GOTCHA! THAT WAS A HUNTER'S TRICK! HA HA!
OH, NO, DRAT. YOU'RE REALLY TO SMART! MERCY! MERCY!
YOU'RE PRETTY WEIRD FOR A FROG.
MY NAME IS ERNEST. I'M A MICROBE, AND YOU'VE CAUGHT ME.
AAATCHOOO!
YOU'RE OBLIVIOUS, SELFISH, AND IRRESPONSIBLE! INCAPABLE OF BABYSITTING!
BUT I'M TELLING YOU I'M SORRY!
YIKES! IT'S CRAZY HERE! DO THEY ALWAYS ARGUE LIKE THAT?
ALL THE TIME...

Don’t miss ERNEST & REBECCA #1 “My Best Friend is a Germ”
coming November 2011!